3800 19 0010600 0

HIGH LIFE HIGHLAND

V&Q
BOOKS

D1471999

Isabel Bogdan was born in Cologne and studied English and Japanese. She is an enthusiastic Hamburg-dweller, reader, writer and translator into German (including Jane Gardam, Jonathan Safran Foer, Nick Hornby, Jasper Fforde). Her first book *Sachen Machen* came out in 2012, followed in 2016 by *The Peacock*, and in 2019 by *Laufen*. She has won prizes for her translating, her writing and the online interview project "Was machen die da?"

Annie Rutherford champions poetry and translated literature in all its guises. She works as Programme Co-ordinator for StAnza, Scotland's international poetry festival, and as a writer and translator. Her published translations include German/Swiss poet Nora Gomringer's *Hydra's Heads* (Burning Eye Books, 2018) and Belarusian poet Volha Hapeyeva's *In My Garden of Mutants* (Arc, 2021). She co-founded the literary magazine *Far Off Places* and Göttingen's Poetree festival.

The Peacock

Isabel Bogdan

Translated from the German by Annie Rutherford

HIGHLAND
LIBRARIES

WITHDRAWN

Co-funded by the Creative Europe
programme of the European Union

V&Q Books, Berlin 2021
An imprint of Verlag Voland & Quist GmbH
First published in the German language as *Der Pfau* by Isabel Bogdan

© 2016 Verlag Kiepenheuer & Witsch GmbH & Co. KG, Cologne/Germany
All rights reserved

Translation copyright © Annie Rutherford
Editing: Katy Derbyshire
Copy editing: Angela Hirons
Cover photo © Dorit Guenter
Cover design: Pingundpong*Gestaltungsbüro
Typesetting: Fred Uhde
Printing and binding: PBtisk, Příbram, Czech Republic

ISBN: 978-3-86391-293-2

www.vq-books.eu

For Jeannie and Hector Maclean

One of the peacocks had gone mad. Or maybe he just couldn't see very well. At any rate, he suddenly regarded anything blue and shiny as competition on the marriage market.

Luckily, there were very few blue and shiny things in the little glen at the foot of the Highlands. There were fields and meadows and trees and altogether a great deal of green, and there was the heather. And any number of sheep. The only shiny blue things which occasionally strayed there were the holidaymakers' cars. Lord and Lady McIntosh had converted the former farm buildings, barns and anything else vaguely suitable which belonged to their estate into holiday cottages, so that the old place recovered at least some of the money it gobbled up. The oldest parts of the castle presumably dated back to the seventeenth century, when the castle had been built, and there had been various annexes and extensions over the following centuries. There hadn't always been enough money for ongoing modernisations, and this remained the case today. The house cost money. The plaster would flake off the facade and need replacing, and then a water pipe would burst, or the roof would need repairing. Lady Fiona mainly repaired the electrics herself, because hardly any electricians nowadays can still cope with 110 volts or deal with the old fuses. The heating costs regularly brought the McIntoshes out in a sweat, which is more than could be said of the temperatures in the house. The ground floor was paved with flagstones, so it was never particularly warm, even in hot summers, and hot summers were rare. In winter it was even colder. There was a central heating system which didn't deserve the name, and so most rooms were simply cold. Only the kitchen was always pleasant, with a fire burning constantly in the old Aga. Almost all year round, the Laird and Lady spent their evenings by the fireplace in the library, where they read, worked or watched DVDs. In winter they sometimes wore woolly hats to bed. They didn't mind, they were used to it. When they were frozen through, they took a bath or got into the hot tub outside on the great lawn.

Lord McIntosh sometimes joked that he might as well go ahead and try to insulate the house with banknotes. The Laird was a classics scholar and didn't understand much about buildings. The Lady was an engineer and understood rather more, despite working for a wind turbine company. They'd both mastered the basics of addition and subtraction. They weren't poor, they had more than enough to live on but not enough for a thorough renovation of the old property.

The cottages had only slightly more modern facilities – they were somewhat better insulated and had carpets and low ceilings, so they were considerably easier to heat. And of course, every bed had an electric blanket. It was really quite cosy in the former gatehouse a mile and a half away by the entrance to the drive, in the gardener's house on the other side of the wee river, in the washhouse half a mile up the glen, in the former stables beyond the woods, and in the other cottages dotted around further away in the glen, next to gravel roads or at the ends of muddy tracks. You visited your next-door neighbours by car here, and if you were drunk on the way home, it didn't matter too much because you were unlikely to meet another car or get pulled over. If you landed in a ditch, there were enough tractors which could pull you out again. The so-called village was made up of a handful of houses, a tiny church, and a telephone box nobody had used for years.

Renting out the cottages was going quite well, people loved the peace and quiet and the nature. Getting away from everything, no phone signal, no TV, just the murmur of the stream. They mostly came in the summer, often middle-aged couples who worked long hours back home and would mainly go for walks here, or families with children. Life was less hurried here than in the city. The nearest town was twelve miles away.

In a fit of exuberance one day, Lord McIntosh had purchased five peacocks, three females and two males; he had imagined how pretty it would be when the males strutted around the great lawn in front of the house, fanning out their trains. The less attractive females were to stay quietly in the background, discreetly giving the males a reason to compete and fan their tail feathers in the first place. That's how he'd pictured it. Lord McIntosh was very keen on animals in general, but he didn't understand very much about them. He hadn't counted on the peacocks widening their radius of activity so much that they generally weren't to be seen at all. He also hadn't counted on the fact that, instead, they could be heard very well indeed, their cries echoing through the glen, so that it sounded a bit like a jungle. But the McIntoshes got used to that, and on the whole the peacocks were left to themselves and did as they pleased. And they only fanned their trains during mating season in the spring; after that, they shed the long tail feathers. These only grew back the following spring, which impressed Lady Fiona all over again each year. Nature really was full of marvels! Once a year the peacocks bred somewhere in the wood and had young, most of which didn't survive. Each year one or two made it, and by now there were at least four males and six females, although no one knew the exact number. The Laird only fed the animals occasionally, mainly in the winter when they couldn't find much to eat. Occasionally one of them froze to death somewhere in the woods, and the McIntoshes didn't really understand why, because the peacocks normally gathered in the shed behind the house where they were fed and where it was considerably warmer. The peacocks came to accept the two dogs, Albert and Victoria, or rather the other way round: Albert realised at some point, firstly, that the peacocks fought back and, secondly, that he wasn't allowed to treat them as toys anyway, and Victoria was too small and too old to even think of such a thing. At some point the peacocks even settled on the division of feed and on social niceties with the cantankerous old goose, and after a while, all of the animals got on and basically left one another alone. They lived peacefully alongside each other and the holidaymakers were delighted no matter what.

Until one of the peacocks went mad. Or couldn't see very well. Afterwards, of course, it was impossible to find out what the problem was and when it had begun. At any rate, when Mr and Mrs Bakshi arrived at the end of August, nobody could have suspected a thing. The Bakshis had rented one of the cottages for three weeks. They were in the former washhouse and were enchanted and enraptured, saying quite often how good they had it and how delightful everything was and how lucky they were to have ended up here. In all honesty, the cottage wasn't exactly luxurious. There was no shower, just a badly insulated bathtub in which the water always went cold immediately. In the kitchen, the floor sloped so much that the Bakshis felt like they were on a ship the first few days, for the ground was never quite where they expected it to be. But it didn't take long before they got used to the fact that the water never fully ran out of the sink, because the plughole wasn't at the lowest point. Mrs Bakshi could cope with the fact that the oil always ended up on one side of the pan – she found this charming and enchanting too. At some point, they even thought it handy that every grape they dropped rolled into the same corner.

Once a day, Mr Bakshi hosed down the paving slabs in front of the cottage to wash away the goose muck. For reasons no one understood, the goose's favourite place to be was right in front of their door. Mr Bakshi was impressed each day by how much mess a single goose could produce. Lady Fiona McIntosh was a wee bit embarrassed that the goose had to choose the area by the washhouse door, of all places, as her new favourite spot, but the Bakshis assured her it didn't bother them at all. Really, the Lady said, a goose like that wasn't meant to be alone, it wasn't good for the creature. But she didn't want to keep acquiring new geese ad infinitum, just to make sure no one goose was ever alone. So perhaps the goose was just looking for a bit of company.

The Bakshis spent their three weeks mainly doing nothing. They went on a lot of walks – down the drive, past the little gatehouse and through the village, along the side of a field (home, surprisingly enough, to two alpacas), over the small footbridge across the river, back along the riverbank to the next bridge but one, and then back to the house. Or they went up to the left behind the house, passed the ruined chapel, which was hidden somewhat behind a dense thicket of trees, crossed a field of cows, and then arced up to the driveway and made their way back from there. On the way, they picked blackberries or stopped to enjoy the views of the hilly landscape and the Highlands up to the north. They opened gates and stepped in cowpats, climbed over fences and stepped in sheep droppings; they rinsed their shoes in the stream which ran through the valley and washed their hands in it. They marvelled at the sheer number of rabbits, went birdwatching and once even saw a magnificent stag. On a particularly warm day, Lady Fiona showed them a place hidden by trees behind a field of cows where the stream was wider, forming a natural pool which they could swim in. It was cold but beautiful – by swimming gently against the current, you could stay in the same place. The Bakshis laughed with pleasure, dried themselves off swiftly afterwards and got dressed.

Otherwise they read and they watched the goose and the peacocks strutting across the lawn. Mr Bakshi crept persistently after the peacocks trying to photograph them, which turned out to be bafflingly tricky, and Mrs Bakshi crocheted a blanket for the grandchild they were expecting soon, their first.

They were so delighted by everything that on their final evening they invited the McIntoshes to a farewell dinner in the wash-house, at which Mrs Bakshi served the Laird and Lady a spectacular chicken korma. It wasn't really the done thing to visit the cottages of paying guests, but since the death of the old Laird a few years ago, Hamish and Fiona McIntosh no longer stood on ceremony.

Nonetheless, Lord McIntosh wanted to first of all deal with some formalities that evening. The tourist board was carrying out a statistical survey and all holidaymakers were meant to fill in a questionnaire: how long they'd been in the area, how often they'd been before, how old they were, what sort of accommodation they'd stayed in and so on. A never-ending questionnaire, which Lady Fiona – as the Laird told the Bakshis – sometimes filled in herself, instead of bothering visitors with it. If needs be, she simply made something up. He didn't think much of this approach, he admitted, but his wife could be almost unstoppable sometimes and was very creative.

Well then, give it here, said Mr Bakshi, and took the questionnaire off the Laird. Mrs Bakshi said people wouldn't fill it in any more honestly than Lady Fiona anyway, so he needn't worry about it. She herself basically ticked whatever she found funniest in this sort of thing or wrote down some kind of nonsense. Lady Fiona McIntosh considered this sensible. The ladies felt they understood each other.

Mr Bakshi read out the questions and asked his wife why they had come here and what they had done during their stay. She asked what the options were; there, she said, *wildlife watching* – that sounded super, that's what they were here for! They really had seen an owl the other night, she said. Yes, the Laird said, you saw them quite often here. And this, said Mrs Bakshi, *action and adventure*, another good one! He should tick that too. Indeed, Mr Bakshi told the McIntoshes, they had experienced both of these things that morning – plenty of *action and adventure* with *wildlife*, right here in the cottage.

That morning, they explained, they had been woken by a strange noise. Mrs Bakshi had thought it must be birds frolicking about outside on the windowsill, perhaps beating the glass with their wings while they, well, made little baby birds. She had got up and carefully drawn the curtains aside and indeed, there was a blue tit there – not outside the window though, but rather on the inside. It was fluttering against the windowpane in a desperate attempt to get out. The Bakshis asked themselves how the blue tit could have got in, all the windows had been closed overnight. Less for fear of birds than of midges. Lord McIntosh said that sometimes birds actually fell down the chimney and made quite a mess with all the soot they brought in with them. The blue tit looked quite clean though, the Bakshis said. Oh well, at any rate it had been inside, in their bedroom. Mrs Bakshi had pushed open the window, and the blue tit had understood pretty quickly, had fluttered onto the windowsill and then out into the woods. Mrs Bakshi had gone back to bed and left the window open to let in a bit of fresh air.

Not a particularly exciting story in itself, but an hour later they awoke to the same sound again. Stupid creature, flying right back in here, Mr Bakshi had grunted into his pillow. But this time it was a swallow, he told the McIntoshes, and tragically it had got stuck between the two panes of the opened window. It took quite a bit of effort to manoeuvre it out, for the creature had panicked, and when they moved the window, it just got its wings stuck even more. In the end, they used the handle of a wooden spoon to somehow push the bird – by now totally distressed – up between the windowpanes. Mr Bakshi was finally able to catch it and put it on the windowsill, where it flew away out into the air – luckily it wasn't injured. But it really was peculiar, the Bakshis said, that two birds had behaved so strangely on one and the same morning, just flying into a human dwelling like that. They didn't normally do that.

Lord McIntosh told them that for a while now a pair of eagles had been nesting somewhere further up in the mountains and that occasionally you could see the eagles from here, mainly far away, high up in the sky. But it did sometimes happen that they came closer and then the birds in the glen always went quite mad. Perhaps that had been the case that morning. First a blue tit mysteriously getting into the house and then a swallow getting stuck between the windowpanes – birds didn't normally act that oddly.

And so the conversation rippled along and they talked about birds while eating Mrs Bakshi's delicious chicken korma. Mr and Mrs Bakshi found it all unbelievably interesting and wonderful to be so close to nature, and Hamish and Fiona were pleased their holidaymakers were so happy.

It was at the end of that evening that the peacock went crazy for the first time. Mr and Mrs Bakshi accompanied the McIntoshes to the door, and when they opened it, the light from the hallway fell on the Bakshis' car. It was metallic blue, glinted in the light and was, to put it mildly, not exactly a luxury vehicle. The four of them were standing by the door and exchanging courtesies when suddenly, as if out of nowhere, one of the peacocks lunged at the car and attacked the vehicle, crying loudly and beating its wings, hammering with a terrible clatter at the hood with its beak, and baffling and startling the McIntoshes just as much as the Bakshis. No one wants to mess with an angry peacock and this one was clearly quite furious. The ladies fled into the cottage and the men had them pass out a blanket, which they shook, yelling at the peacock. This apparently impressed him sufficiently and he flapped away.

The Bakshis and the McIntoshes first of all drank a whisky for the fright. And then another. And then they stopped, because Lady Fiona was, after all, a Lady. Before the McIntoshes left, they turned off the light in the cottage so as not to illuminate the blue car and tempt the angry peacock back again.

The damage to the car, it turned out the next morning, was considerable. The peacock had achieved quite a lot in the short space of time; the car bonnet had dents in it, and the paint was chipped in several places. Mr Bakshi said it wasn't so bad, his workshop would be able to fix it, and anyway his wife had been saying for years that he really ought to buy a new car. But, well, Mr Bakshi said, he was somehow rather fond of the old thing.

There you go then, said the Laird, for that very reason he'd simply run it through his own insurance. He wanted to cover the damages, of course – and on top of that, the Bakshis were welcome to stay for free in the former washhouse for two weeks next year – that's if they dared to come back after this attack. He was sure the peacock would have calmed down by then. Who knew, maybe he had been disturbed by the eagle's presence too? Why this would cause him to attack a car, the Laird wasn't sure, but who knew what kind of displacement activities a peacock was capable of?

And so the two couples said goodbye with all kinds of assurances that it really wasn't that bad – the insurance would sort it out, and they'd certainly come to an agreement, and Mr Bakshi should definitely send them the bill, and they'd be delighted to see each other next year.

All of this happened in mid-September. In October, the peacock tore a blue rubbish bag to shreds and spread its contents spaciously across the lawn; took a visiting child's blue toy away and carried it off into the woods where it couldn't be found, so that Hamish had to pacify the distraught child with a somewhat larger present in red; and smashed, with considerable noise, the decorative blue ceramic sphere which Fiona had placed next to the pond, hacking it into a thousand little shards.

At the start of November, the little old dog, Victoria, died and was buried in the woods. Albert and the McIntoshes were grieving and had other things on their minds than dealing with the crazy peacock. One day the blue plastic water butt had holes and tears in it and started leaking, while a friend of the McIntoshes was only just able to park his car in the garage in time. Ryszard rescued the blue plastic sheet covering the springs of the trampoline, which stood in a corner of the great lawn, by concealing it under a green sheet. Ryszard, a young Pole, was responsible for everything that went on outdoors. Innumerable acres of land belonged to the estate, almost half the glen, and this land had to be looked after. Ryszard took care of the heather, the woods and the fields; he patched fences, serviced the electrical lines to the cottages, dug ditches with the digger, used machinery to remove fallen trees, and chopped them up to be used as firewood. He also cared for the great lawn in front of the house and dealt with anything technical which Lady Fiona couldn't manage herself. Ryszard was a great help to Lord and Lady McIntosh and even something of a relief after a few unpleasant experiences with his predecessors. Ryszard could see for himself what needed to be done, he enjoyed working and he worked hard. He didn't talk much, for even after a few years in Scotland, his English wasn't particularly good. He was reserved but always friendly and reliable.

By now it was clear that it wasn't the eagle which so enraged the peacock, but the colour blue. The peacock was still young and had clearly reached the onset of puberty – he had only recently grown his blue plumage and his train still wasn't particularly long – and the McIntoshes assumed that this was all some kind of adolescent hormonal confusion. The only blue thing the bird didn't attack was the other peacocks. They were also the only things which fought back. The mating season was over, but they hadn't noticed the peacock acting strangely then. Nobody knew whether he had mated successfully, and something must have gone wrong. The McIntoshes decided to wait and see whether the problem would clear up on its own over the winter and, if they had the chance, to ask for the vet's advice. At the moment they just didn't have time to deal with it – they were expecting important guests.

The management of the investment department of a London private bank had rented the entire west wing for a long weekend at the end of November. The head of the department was travelling with four colleagues, a cook and a psychologist, for *Creative Time-Out and Teambuilding Activities* – as it was called. Creative, complained Hamish McIntosh, why do bankers need to be creative, thank you very much, perhaps to doctor balance sheets? The McIntoshes sensed from the very first telephone calls with the department secretary (who wouldn't be coming herself) that the head of the investment department could be somewhat difficult. But she was bringing money. And so they were busy doing up the west wing, for it might have been pretty luxurious a hundred years ago, but that was a hundred years ago. And it was about that long since anyone had come here with their own cook too.

Aileen was doing overtime. Aileen was the housekeeper and cleaner for the big house and the cottages. She did the family's laundry and changed the sheets in the holiday homes, she put out tea and biscuits when new guests arrived, and she had pretty clear ideas about what was necessary, what needed to be done and what was entirely superfluous. In short, Aileen kept the show on the road. One day she would be an excellent homemaker, but after a few short catastrophic relationships, just now she was happy on her own. She still had plenty of time to have weans, and she wasn't worried about finding the right man to start a family. He just needed to be peaceable, not drink too much and have a job – her requirements weren't all that exacting. She would continue to work too, of course – she enjoyed being the mistress of several cottages and all that belonged to them.

Aileen informed Hamish that a new shower unit for the bathroom in the west wing was essential. They really couldn't subject guests to the trickle of that old lukewarm shower any more, certainly not such important guests. Hamish generally did what Aileen said, for she was considerably more practically minded than he was and so he had a new shower unit installed, one which produced unlimited amounts of really hot water. Not much could be done about the water pressure unfortunately –

the old pipes simply didn't allow for more pressure. But a hot trickle of a shower was still better than a lukewarm one.

Over time, quite a lot of junk had accumulated in the west wing. It was quite big and only rarely rented out, so the McIntoshes stored all sorts of things there when they couldn't otherwise decide what to do with them. Boxes of books and the grownup children's discarded toys, pieces of furniture they no longer used but which were either too nice to throw away or simply hadn't been disposed of yet, crockery, vases, Christmas decorations, worn-out rugs, antlers, paintings and all the other things found in old houses which have been passed down from generation to generation and which nobody ever moves out of. Aileen sorted through some stuff, took this or that bit of broken furniture to the dump, and put everything else in the garage for now. It would be kept dry and out of the way there – and the garage door could simply be shut. Which of course didn't solve the actual problem but merely relocated it. Some of the old things ought to be taken to the charity shop, and Aileen knew perfectly well that each time everything was sorted through and moved, it would prompt the Laird to part with a few more things. In that sense, this was at least a step in the right direction. And above all, the west wing could now be rented out again.

Aileen took down the long, dark red velvet curtains and took them to the dry-cleaners because they wouldn't fit in any washing machine. She shampooed the carpets in the entire west wing, cleaned the windows, and checked inside all of the wardrobes and dresser drawers to make sure nothing had been left behind by a previous visitor, or in case the odd moth had died in any of them. She even cleaned the glass of the old framed prints. In some of them, colonies of tiny insects had settled between the picture and the glass. The print *The Weighing of the Birds* was particularly bad. She took it down and carried it to the laundry room so as to clean it in peace later. There were advantages to these important people coming, she thought. She could finally clean as thoroughly as she'd been wanting to do for ages. Really, she should have taken all the pictures down and out of their frames and removed the insects, but she didn't have the time. At least the picture with the worst infestation ought to look alright, particularly given that it hung so prominently, right next to the front door. What even were these creatures which lived in the picture frames? she asked herself. What did they live off? Such infinitesimally wee bits of paper that you couldn't even spot the damage when you looked? Dust? All that could be seen were tiny spots, which presumably came from the animals' excretions. And where did the beasties come from anyway, how did they get into the frames? Aileen removed the tiny minibeasts with a paintbrush. The print showed a shooting party which was weighing the pheasants and grouse they had shot, on a large set of scales.

Two days before the bankers were due to arrive, the picture was hanging in its place again. The glass was now considerably cleaner than that of the other pictures, making the dirt on the rest of them even more conspicuous, but Aileen couldn't take all the other pictures out of their frames to clean the inside of the glass now. Simply removing all the pictures wasn't an option either, because there were large pale marks on the wallpaper behind them.

Aileen made the beds and laid out sufficient towels. When, last of all, she tried to blow and shake the dust off some old dried flowers, the posy disintegrated completely. The dried petals fluttered to the floor and Aileen had to fetch Henry again. Henry was the hoover, a small, round, red appliance with a painted smiling face. The hoover tube was attached to Henry's nose, like a trunk. All the cottages had Henrys too, and the friendly vacuum cleaners always made Aileen smile. She was on the whole a cheerful soul and was generally good-humoured. She was in a particularly good mood today. She had taken a radio with her into the west wing and was singing along to it at the top of her voice. She and Henry cut a mean figure as they danced across the carpet to Abba – *You can dance, you can jive, having the time of your...* And then she got an awful shock because suddenly Lady Fiona was standing in the doorway with her arms crossed, watching her with amusement. Aileen turned Henry and the radio off and stammered, gosh, that had startled her! How long had the Lady been standing there? Lady Fiona grinned, said, Och, and told her that the driver from the dry-cleaners had been and had delivered the curtains, and could Aileen come and help her carry them?

The two women lugged the metres of thick velvet into the west wing and hung up the curtains. Aileen stood at the top of the stepladder, the Lady passed her the heavy curtains and both of them were pleased but a little ashamed at how magnificent the curtains now looked and how necessary it had clearly been.

The postie tooted his horn at the front of the house. Lady Fiona left to see to him, and Aileen turned the radio on again. It might be a while before the Lady returned, but she couldn't hang up the next curtain on her own, it was too heavy. She inspected the bathroom once more to see if there was anything left to do there, and she tested the new shower. She sang along to the radio somewhat less loudly this time, worried Lady Fiona might overhear her again. The water was at least nice and warm now, but it trickled out of the showerhead as meekly as it ever had. Ach well, she decided. That wasn't her problem. If the bankers had an issue with it, then that was their bad luck. Maybe a wee bit less luxury would even do them some good. Aileen didn't have a particularly high opinion of bankers.

The next curtains to hang up were the ones in the living room. Aileen took the stepladder through, and then *Come on Eileen* came on the radio. Her song! Aileen began singing at the top of her voice again, chose the ladder as her dance partner this time, and reeled with it through the living room, where her previous partner, Henry, presented an unfortunate trip hazard. Maybe he was jealous. A leg of the stepladder got caught in the hoover tube, and Aileen stumbled and fell, along with the ladder, on top of Henry. She heard a crack in her right arm. The pain was overwhelming. Dazed, she remained on the ground until Lady Fiona came back; freed her from the tangle of the grinning Henry, his cable, the hoover tube and the stepladder; turned off the – in Aileen's words – *goddamn bloody radio*; and called an ambulance. It didn't take a doctor to recognise that Aileen's arm was broken.

It took a while for the ambulance to drive the fifteen miles from the hospital into the glen. Aileen made it into an armchair with the help of the Lady. Her arm now lay on a cushion on top of the armrest, and it hurt so much that tears kept welling up in her eyes. Lady Fiona prescribed her a painkiller. She also offered her a whisky, but Aileen didn't want one, she didn't drink – ever – and Fiona McIntosh knew that. Anyway, it was possible that she might need an operation, and in that case it certainly wouldn't be a good idea to arrive at the hospital drunk. The Lady promised to look after Aileen's dog, Britney, until she got out of hospital. And yes, she would also look by Aileen's cottage a few miles up the glen, would water the flowers and check the post. Aileen's parents had moved into town a few years previously, after her father's driving licence was revoked when he was caught drink-driving yet again. In town he could use public transport to get around and didn't need to be constantly chauffeured by his wife. Since then, Aileen had lived alone in her parents' house. At the time, she'd been working in a restaurant along the road to the next village and saw no reason to move away with her parents. Quite the contrary, she was old enough to live alone and was pretty happy to. She loved the glen and the house. She had had a thorough clear-out, painted everything in light colours, and made a cosy, bright home out of the gloomy and cluttered cottage. She pitied her father for his alcohol consumption and her mother for putting up with it and for being just as powerless against it as her father was. But Aileen couldn't help her parents out of the situation either and now only had sporadic contact with them.

Anyway, said Lady Fiona, Aileen definitely wouldn't have to stay in hospital long with a broken arm – she would probably get a plaster cast and then be sent back home. Aileen should simply call when she wanted picked up. And Fiona was sure Ryszard would be happy to take care of the cottages while Aileen's arm was in plaster.

Oh yes, he'd manage, Lady Fiona assured Aileen. Yes, he'd cope with the cleaning too. Secretly she wasn't quite so sure, for in all honesty she was just as convinced as Aileen that no one could clean as well as Aileen did, but she reassured her as best she could. Aileen had a soft spot for Ryszard, he was big and strong and hardworking and kind, and he loved nature. But as far as cleaning was concerned, she didn't trust him much at all. Aileen would never have admitted the former, but she was quite frank with the Lady about the latter. Lady Fiona confessed that she wasn't really convinced of Ryszard's cleaning talents either, she considered him more of a handyman, but she'd certainly come up with some kind of solution. Aileen wasn't to worry about it and was to give her arm time to heal. If necessary, Lady Fiona would simply dance through the cottages with Henry herself. Aileen didn't quite know whether she was allowed to laugh at this image or whether Lady Fiona would be offended, so she concentrated instead on dictating to the Lady what still needed to be done: which cottage had a broken kettle, where the cutlery drawer needed to be refilled, and which beds needed to be made up. Luckily, the cottages weren't all continuously occupied at this time of year, so one or other of them could go a few days without being cleaned. Being able to at least think about work distracted her, and when the charming paramedics arrived, Aileen almost felt up to flirting. If only it weren't for the pain.

Subsequently, Lady Fiona McIntosh was doing overtime too. She could have done without Aileen breaking her arm right now – various bits and pieces still needed to be done in the west wing, and Aileen was simply more practiced at that kind of thing.

Frustratingly enough, Aileen's arm was put in an impressive plaster, and she was sent straight back home, where she couldn't even open the front door, because to do so you had to hold and turn the key with one hand and turn the handle with the other. Lady Fiona decided on the spot that Aileen should come and stay with her for now. Without the use of her right arm, she was in rather a fix after all. So instead of Aileen looking after the west wing and Fiona McIntosh developing a concept for a new wind farm, Fiona was instead looking after Aileen, the west wing and her own household, and developing the wind farm concept on top of that. Really her work should have required her complete attention. She normally started getting ready for Christmas around now too – Lady Fiona was very organised when it came to that sort of thing – but this year it would have to wait. When the children came home before Christmas they'd just have to help. They'd never known it any other way, everyone always had to pitch in around here.

Lady Fiona had got one of the children's old rooms ready for Aileen, and together they fetched some clothes and everything else Aileen needed from her cottage. Then they went into the west wing, and Aileen explained in detail what still needed to be done. She apologised at least a thousand times for breaking her arm and stressed how embarrassed she was that she was now giving the Lady instructions instead of the other way round. Lady Fiona countered that Aileen presumably hadn't broken her arm on purpose, so it wasn't her fault and she should stop apologising. It wasn't as if Fiona hadn't ever cleaned or done any other kind of work herself, so it really was all absolutely fine. And of course Aileen knew that Lady Fiona didn't think such menial tasks beneath her, she used to cope without her after all. She had cleaned and rented out the cottages alongside her work, had managed the whole estate, and had brought up the children on top of that. Back then she'd only worked part-time though. The fact that she was long since back in full-time work as a senior engineer commanded Aileen's total respect. Aileen might have been 25 years younger than the Lady, but in many ways she was considerably more conservative. She had assumed for a surprisingly long time that Lady Fiona's main job was being a lady – but that was before she worked for her, when she only knew her in passing, the way you know a person who lives in the same glen.

And then it was Thursday already. The manager of the London private bank's investment department and her Irish setter arrived in a brand-new, metallic blue sports car, while the rest of the group drove up in sedate black. With her very first step out of the blue car, the investment department manager trod in some goose muck. She was, of course, still wearing her elegant city shoes and, of course, wasn't overly amused; in fact, she was extremely vexed. Long car journeys didn't exactly relax her, and she could hardly be said to have a relaxed attitude at the best of times. She made an effort to maintain her composure, but really she was of the opinion that when guests arrived, the property owners should make sure there was no excrement lying around where they'd have to park, thank you very much. While she was still trying to wipe the worst of it off on the lawn, the goose waddled towards her at surprising speed, gobbling noisily with its neck outstretched towards her. Few people tended to consider the goose's greeting as particularly friendly. She had never hurt anyone, but her aggressive demeanour thoroughly startled most people. The goose was certainly a considerably better guard dog than Albert, who did usually bark when greeting guests but wagged his tail with joy while doing so. The investment department manager would never have admitted to being scared of a goose, but to be honest, the attack hardly improved her mood and merely confirmed her reservations against such large birds. She had had a fright and quite an adrenaline surge and had broken out in a sweat. She was a little scared of the goose, had goose muck on one of her expensive shoes, and on top of everything else, it was damn cold. This was off to a great start!

The McIntoshes automatically shooed away the goose and didn't find her droppings worthy of further remark or in any way tragic. This was the countryside, after all. Anyone who came here came for that very reason. If not specifically for the goose muck. The McIntoshes were considerably more concerned about the manager's blue car, but they couldn't very well say so. They could see that the lady wasn't particularly well disposed towards birds just now, even if she was trying to be polite. So they began by welcoming the bankers warmly and offered up the garden hose and some kitchen roll for the manager to remedy the mishap on her shoe. She took a few steps to the side and almost stumbled over a dead animal, which immediately gave her yet another fright.

The animal wasn't dead; it was a toy monkey which Albert and Victoria had loved to bits, almost literally. Since Victoria's death a few weeks ago, Albert had acted out his grief on the monkey in particular, but, of course, the investment department manager couldn't know that. She also didn't know whether she was more disgusted by the goose muck on her shoe or by the dead monkey. Her own dog noticed the cuddly toy with considerably more enthusiasm, and the manager promptly forbade him from playing with it. The dog didn't listen. He was called Mervyn, like the former head of the Bank of England, which might have been a coincidence but it did give the McIntoshes cause to hope that the woman might possess something like a sense of humour after all. The psychologist, the cook and the rest of the bankers stood nearby awkwardly and tried to make small talk.

The McIntoshes enquired politely about whether the group had found the place alright and whether it had been a pleasant journey. While Lady Fiona was showing the group around (and Albert was showing Mervyn everything outside), the Laird excused himself for a moment and went to look for Ryszard. To be sure, there hadn't been any more incidents with the peacock for a few weeks. The whole thing had probably blown over a while ago, but it was possible that there simply hadn't been any blue things around. Better to be on the safe side. Unfortunately, they couldn't ask the manager to put her car in the garage, because all the crates, cases and bits of furniture from the west wing were being stored there.

There was no phone signal, so Hamish couldn't simply call Ryszard, but luckily they had discussed what needed to be done that day not long before the bankers had arrived. Ryszard had planned to first deal with a blocked drain in one of the cottages before finishing some tasks in the woods, where the devastation caused by the latest storm hadn't quite been cleared away yet. Lord McIntosh got into the car and hoped he would find Ryszard still at the cottage, but he was already finished there, and the drainpipe was fixed. The young family staying in the holiday home was full of praise for the swift – and so friendly – resolution of their problem. They offered Lord McIntosh a cup of tea and were clearly in the mood for a chat. He thanked them but refused, explaining that he really did need to find Ryszard quite urgently. This might be tricky, hopefully he hadn't disappeared into the depths of the woods. Lord McIntosh didn't have an overview of exactly what needed to be done in which part of in the woods, he only knew the vague direction and he wasn't in the four-wheel-drive, just the normal car, so he'd have to stick to the road. The bankers were sure to wonder why the Laird had driven away so suddenly instead of taking his time to greet them and show them around – and on top of all this, there was the very real danger that the peacock might launch itself upon the investment department manager's car without delay, and she was already less than happy about the goose and its droppings.

All this made him thoroughly nervous. Luckily, Ryszard had run into one of the farmers from the glen on his way to the devastated woods and had pulled in briefly, so Hamish met him while he was still on the road. He asked Ryszard to tempt the peacocks far away from the house with some feed or something; he didn't want to see them over the next few days, he said – Madame had arrived in a blue car.

Ryszard promised to deal with it.

The group from London was settling into the west wing. The single room, announced the investment department manager, was for her, the others would all have to pair up and share.

All four men hurried so as to be sure that they wouldn't have to put their suitcases in the room with the double bed. It was bad enough that they had to share a room; having to sleep in the same bed as a colleague was out of the question – for all of them. The cook and the psychologist looked at each other, the cook rolled her eyes and the psychologist shrugged her shoulders. Rachel hadn't counted on having to share not only a room but also a bed with a stranger around thirty years older than her, but if that's the way things were then that's the way things were. The cook seemed quite friendly, and the bed was wide enough. Rachel had other things to worry about this weekend.

Jim and Andrew had a room with twin beds and spotted the electric blankets straight away. Jim wasn't particularly bothered, but Andrew eyed them with secret glee, although he didn't show it. Jim didn't feel the cold, he'd grown up in modest circumstances and hadn't exactly been spoilt with warmth as a child. Besides, he was easily satisfied by nature, he tended to take things as they came. This had worked out pretty well for him over the past sixty years. Andrew was the opposite really, easily rattled when things didn't go according to his expectations, and he was already deeply sceptical about this whole weekend. He wasn't happy at the sight of the sagging bed but was glad to find the electric blanket, for it really was quite cold. He kept that to himself though, as was his way. Andrew didn't speak about his inner conflicts. Jim didn't have any.

David and Bernard had bunk beds in the next room, which Bernard wasn't pleased about at all. He didn't want to sleep in either the upper or the lower bunk, because he couldn't decide whether he'd rather crash onto the sleeping David below, together with the entire upper bunk, or risk sleeping below David and being killed by him and the falling bed. Either way he was afraid of bunk beds, but he decided he'd rather sleep in the upper bunk after all, because he'd feel claustrophobic in the lower one. On top of all this, he'd been finding it tough enough sleeping alone since his breakup. Sharing a room with a colleague would surely make it even worse. He didn't mind, he claimed patronisingly, he was happy to sleep in the upper bunk. David didn't care as long as there was an electric blanket in his bed, and as long as Bernard didn't notice him using it. Bernard would definitely make fun of him, but David was simply freezing.

Bernard continued to grumble. Nobody had told him they'd have to share a room, he moaned, and now this. Honestly, bunk beds, they were most definitely past that age! Besides, it was bloody cold. David didn't say much, as usual. He took his slippers out of his suitcase, and Bernard asked snippily whether he was planning on moving in here, it looked as if he was making himself at home. He was of the opinion, he added, that they were here to work, and they could make that clear by adhering to the usual dress code. Although he had expected a proper hotel with a few more conveniences.

A similar scene had just taken place next door, where Jim had taken off his sports jacket to replace it with a baggy knitted jumper, and Andrew had silently thought to himself that this did seem a little unprofessional. He didn't remark on it though,

34

instead chatting about the landscape and the view from the window. At the same time, he envied Jim for his lack of self-consciousness in such matters – but personally he simply felt more at ease when he was dressed properly. Particularly in this rather tense atmosphere, which admittedly had very little to do with Jim.

In both rooms the men realised, with some very quiet but occasionally rather coarse curses, that the radiators barely produced any heat at all and that it was and would remain damn cold in the bedrooms despite the extra electric fan heaters. Which was hardly surprising, given that the entire wing was generally empty and therefore also unheated, as Lady Fiona had been quick to explain.

Liz, the investment department manager, called into the men's rooms that one of the two bathrooms would be for the ladies, namely the one with the new shower unit, which the Lady had pointed out to them. The other, with a bath and no shower, was for the men, she said. So they were going to have to take baths. They'd have to discuss whose turn was when, because the boiler only ever heated enough water for one bath, and after that it needed a few hours to heat the next load. The Lady had explained that too. Andrew asked why they couldn't have just gone to a normal hotel, where everyone would have had their own room with a proper mattress and their own bathroom. Because, the head of the investment department snapped back, then he'd have just spent the whole day playing around on his smartphone again instead of participating in the teambuilding. She had specifically told her secretary to look for a location without a connection to civilisation. Andrew went pale. Nobody had told him there wasn't any phone signal here either. And even Liz thought it didn't need to be quite this primitive.

Andrew helped Helen, the cook, to carry in her things. She had brought whole boxes of provisions with her, because nobody had been able to tell her in advance precisely how far it was to the nearest supermarket. Jim went into the kitchen too, hoping for something to eat, picked up an apple and then helped Rachel, the psychologist, to bring her facilitation equipment into the sitting room. Rachel hadn't parked her car with the others at the side of the house, because there wasn't enough space, so she'd parked behind the house instead, next to a small shed. The peacocks, which had been on the big lawn in front of the house, were now here too; there was probably too much bustle for them round the front at the moment. Rachel carried her things – the facilitator's toolbox, display boards, flipcharts and so on – from the car to the front door, where Jim took them off her and carried them into the sitting room. That way they brought less dirt into the west wing. Each time he appeared at the door, Jim had something to eat in his hand – an apple, a chocolate bar, a slice of toast.

David came out to help too but then got into conversation with Lady Fiona, who was still standing by the door, keeping an eye on Albert and Mervyn as they played on the lawn. At least, that's what it looked like. Actually, she was making sure the peacock didn't attack the investment department manager's car before Ryszard was able to lure the birds away. In an unobserved moment, she had put some feed in the bucket in the shed so that the birds would at least stay back there for now.

Bernard was the only one who didn't come out to help. Helping the ladies was taking things a step too far, he thought. The teambuilding stuff was the psychologist's business, the stuff for the kitchen was the cook's business. He was a banker, not a handyman. He stayed in his room, unpacked his suitcase, hung his shirts on the hodgepodge of hangers, and folded everything else into neat piles in the drawers. In one half of them. David would, of course, want to unpack his things too and to use the other half of the wardrobe. Bernard found this downright degrading. He left his underwear in the suitcase – that really would be too much, putting his underclothes next to those of a colleague.

Rachel went back to the car and fetched a box filled with paper in different colours, and a sheet of blue tissue paper floated out of the car. She had her hands full, so she left it on the ground for now and carried her things to the door. When she came back, one of the peacocks had got hold of the blue tissue paper and was tearing it into shreds. Rachel was astonished – the bird seemed downright furious with the paper. Then she remembered she had once read about a peacock which had screamed at its own reflection, mistaking it for a rival. Maybe peacocks were a little simple. Heaven knows what this one had against the paper! Before she knew it, it had torn the sheet into tiny pieces, which were drifting in all directions. Rachel tried to gather up a few of the bigger scraps without getting too close to the furious bird. Then she got the final things out of her car and locked it, thinking to herself that this was probably unnecessary, up here where no one ever came. Jim took the things off her and carried them into the house, and she helped Andrew with the last boxes for the kitchen. She didn't say anything about the peacock going crazy. The team's boss had joined them by now, and Rachel figured that she'd already had one strange encounter with a bird on their arrival and probably wouldn't want to hear another odd story about a bird. Besides, the Laird was now back and was telling her and David a bit about the history of the house and the age of the trees on the other side of the lawn.

As soon as Rachel was gone from the back of the house, Ryszard appeared, took the bucket of feed and lured the peacocks away. He didn't see Rachel after that, and he didn't notice the scraps of blue paper. And Rachel didn't see him either.

Andrew joked about what mountains of food you clearly needed for just a few people and a few days, he'd already carried unimaginable quantities of fruit, vegetables and drinks inside, but he added that the cook was clearly a pro, and he was sure she knew what she was doing. She'd also brought a few of her favourite pots and even her own case of knives, he said. Rachel thought to herself that if Jim continued to eat as much as he had so far, then they really would need an awful lot of food. Andrew took the last box with meat in it from Rachel and carried it into the kitchen, a big dining kitchen with an old table, which could seat a good dozen people in the large armchairs around it.

Andrew and Rachel sat down with drinks at the table, while the cook tidied everything into the larder, the fridge and the kitchen cupboards and got down to work on the first evening meal. She thought, and she said as much, that if you wanted to work properly – and they were here to work – then you also needed to eat properly. In the evenings there would always be a proper hot meal with three courses, she said, with something a bit lighter for lunch so they wouldn't be too tired in afternoons. It was too late to enjoy a large meal this evening though, they'd just have some cold cuts, cheese, crackers and several salads, and a soup to start with – nothing special, she said. She'd cooked the soup the day before and brought it with her. Several salads sounded to the bankers like ample work and not particularly appealing, but they didn't yet know Helen.

Helen first of all made tea for everyone and put a few scones and crumpets on the table, as well as butter and jam – all homemade of course, she told Jim when he asked, with the exception of the butter. The men helped themselves enthusiastically. Rachel too ate with relish, only the boss held back, murmuring something about her figure. Rachel suggested holding their first session before dinner and their second one right after it, in order to establish the aims of their stay and compile their personal catalogue on feedback culture.

Jim laid and lit a fire in the stove in the sitting room. Rachel unpacked her facilitator's case, put up the display boards, a flip-chart and a whiteboard, laid out felt tips, whiteboard markers, sticky dots, brightly coloured post-its – some in the shape of funny speech bubbles or clouds – paper and pens. She arranged a few chairs and an armchair into a circle and was looking forward to her first big assignment as a teambuilding coach. Really her boss was meant to have mentored this group, but he had unexpectedly been taken ill. Rachel preferred not to think about the extent to which his illness might be connected to the fact that he knew the investment department manager from his university days and would have liked to refuse the contract from the start but couldn't, for, as he put it, *historical reasons*. Rachel had decided to approach it all with a positive attitude and make the best of things. What could possibly go wrong? Sure, she didn't have all that much experience, but she had the feeling she knew what she was doing. She found the bankers a little weird, but who wasn't? And the McIntoshes' estate and the whole valley were just enchanting, you didn't get that every day. The only problem was that you weren't really meant to do teambuilding with a manager present, only with team members who worked at the same level as each other. But she would make it work.

Ryszard did what he could. He took Albert and the bucket of feed with him, leaving Britney – Aileen's dog, who could be somewhat hysterical at times – at home just in case. Albert was a border collie mix, a sheep dog through and through, and he was in his element. With the clatter of the bucket at the front and the dog barking at the back, they lured and drove the peacocks a good distance through the woods and out into an open field. Ryszard scattered feed generously across the field. He hoped it would keep the birds occupied for a while and they wouldn't return to the big house too quickly. If he did this a few times a day, he thought, the peacocks would probably keep their distance from the house and the blue car until Sunday. At night the birds were always in the woods anyway, roosting somewhere in the trees, and he'd scatter some more feed first thing tomorrow morning. Besides, he didn't think anything would happen anyway, the teenage bird's hormonal confusion had to be over by now. Even a peacock had to grow up at some point, and having done so, he'd be able to mate normally next year instead of throwing himself at everything which was blue. After all, peacocks aren't exactly people. People, thought Ryszard, suffered from hormonal confusion for a remarkably long time. He counted himself in that.

While Helen got dinner ready in the kitchen, Rachel welcomed the participants to their first session and wrote three questions on a flipchart: what is important to me, what am I proud of, what do I wish for? They were to write down their answers to these questions, please, and then share them with the group. However, their answers couldn't have anything to do with work or family.

For a moment, silence reigned. Jim took out his pen and started writing. David went pale. Andrew said quietly: no. Rachel looked at him in surprise, then Bernard too said that surely she wasn't serious, there was no way he'd do that. The boss agreed matter-of-factly with the two men – that really would be too intimate, they were here to talk about their work after all, their private lives were not a matter for discussion. The boss had a particular knack for making her opinion extremely clear.

Rachel was flabbergasted but choked back her reaction and explained that she hadn't wanted to tread on anyone's toes, the point was just to get to know a side of each other that they might not know yet. But, of course, she didn't want anyone to feel uncomfortable, she continued. So instead they were to please draw their company as a ship: with different decks, a navigating bridge, an engine room, and they should position themselves in the correct place and so on.

The bankers rolled their eyes but were too polite for a second mutiny. Rachel took some larger pieces of paper and felt tips in every colour out of her little case, handed round the paper, put the pens in the middle of the table and left the bankers to their fate. She went into the kitchen and flopped into a chair. Helen wordlessly passed her a cup of tea.

When she returned to the living room, everyone had finished their ship except for Jim. Jim had drawn a spaceship and would probably have been happy to work on it for another three hours. At least, that was the impression he gave Rachel as he explained his picture. He had clearly had fun constructing the spaceship, considering the details, bringing in different decks, thinking about the propulsion. He cited Douglas Adams' Bistromathics and the Infinite Improbability Drive and audaciously connected these concepts with the flows of money in the bank and in global finance. Rachel asked where he would position himself. Jim grinned and pointed at the galley. He, he said, was the cook. The spaceship bank could continue travelling without him – he certainly wasn't directly responsible for keeping the machine running – but the role of the cook nonetheless had a certain importance for everyone involved. And indeed, the others all grinned with acknowledgement, even the boss. Rachel then interrupted his presentation of the spaceship because she could already sense that none of the others would really be able to match it.

Andrew had drawn a submarine. He talked about the constant danger of destruction and about the control points in the submarine at which this destruction was prevented, whether by controlling the pressure balance when surfacing, or checking the oxygen content of the available air. He was a surprisingly talented artist and seemed to understand quite a bit about technology too. He had drawn identical figures at all of his control points and said that he would sit at one of these, just like everyone else present, it didn't matter at all which one you wanted to use as a metaphor for whom. Rachel was impressed by both men's creativity.

David had drawn a cargo ship and compared the money the bank managed with the cargo being transported. He had forgotten to draw himself on the ship and couldn't really say off the top of his head where he saw himself. He didn't understand enough about ships for that, he said. Bernard and the boss had both drawn passenger liners and hardly dared to present their ships, because they felt so unimaginative and couldn't really add anything substantial to the thoughts of the others. Both of them had placed the boss on the bridge. Bernard had drawn himself as the pilot. This provoked a general rolling of eyes, which he by no means missed. They were all secretly relieved that they hadn't needed to position the rest of the group too.

Before dinner, the bankers wanted to go on their first short walk. They had been sitting down long enough for the drive here and then again in the sitting room and were looking forward to some fresh air and exercise. Of course, it wasn't any warmer outside than it was in the house, and it was almost dark, but at least they could wrap up warmly and keep moving. Even Bernard and Andrew took off their jackets and wore thick jumpers beneath their winter coats instead.

Liz was the first to have her shoes and coat on, for Mervyn wanted out quite particularly urgently. She opened the door and Mervyn stormed out, barking with satisfaction and startling one of the peacocks which had become separated from the rest of the group. It fluttered onto the roof, slipped on the slanted tiles, slid down backwards and fell off the roof in the very moment that the investment department manager stepped out of the door, missing her head by inches.

It gave Liz a terrible fright. She hadn't noticed Mervyn startling the bird and thought that the whole house was coming down on her head. The bird landed on the ground, wings beating, and Liz let out a scream, which didn't exactly help to calm the peacock, so that it fluttered up again and thankfully disappeared onto the nearest tree. Liz couldn't abide birds. To her mind, the encounter with the cantankerous goose had been quite enough for one day. Behind her, the men didn't see what happened at all, they just heard a cry. Liz didn't want to let her horror show, but beneath her thick winter jacket the adrenaline kick prompted quite an outbreak of sweat. As if she hadn't had enough of that in the past few hours.

The men, of course, noticed that their boss was far from relaxed yet again, but they weren't aware of any reason to feel guilty. They let her go on ahead with Mervyn and talked instead to Rachel, whom David and Jim at least thought quite lovely. Andrew liked her too but wasn't a fan of her working methods. Bernard was in a bad mood either way and was sulking a bit because the ships the others had drawn were so much more creative and elaborate than his own. The boss marched on ahead furiously and first of all tried to make herself calm down. Then she forced herself to walk more slowly so as not to get even more sweaty, as she was already beginning to freeze. The goose emerged out of the bushes and waddled towards her, gobbling and head outstretched. Liz almost stumbled in shock over the stuffed monkey and had yet another adrenaline surge and another outbreak of sweat. She unzipped her jacket a little. She sweated and shivered.

A little way behind the house, the group discovered a large, old ice house, partially embedded into an earth wall. They could hardly make it out in the dusk. Most of them had never seen anything like it before. Jim explained what he knew about ice houses, which turned out to be a surprising amount. They had existed, he said, since the bronze age. In winter, people had stored ice in them for the coming months, and their insulation had been continually improved over the centuries, with wood and straw and air locks and concentric rooms with insulating layers of air between them, so that in the end it was possible even in hot regions to keep food cool throughout the summer and store ice until the next winter. David and Rachel were impressed that such a thing was still in existence today, even if this ice house clearly wasn't in use any more and didn't date back to the bronze age either. Nobody dared to ask precisely when the bronze age actually was. It was more of a simple ice house; there were, as far as they could see, no double walls and no air locks, just a large room embedded into the earth wall. It would certainly be fairly cool there throughout the year, but it was questionable whether you would be able to store ice there in summer. Bernard and the boss both felt that their impression of having landed in the middle ages had been confirmed. More than anything they would have liked to turn around right now and drive straight home, but of course they kept on walking. Liz was freezing.

After just a few hundred metres they came to a gate which even Jim and David's combined strength couldn't open. Bernard muttered that the gate was surely there to keep out some kind of animal, maybe there were wild bulls in the field and wouldn't it be better to turn back? That was nonsense, Jim countered, hadn't he ever been for a walk in the countryside before? It was winter after all, there probably weren't even any cows outside at this time of year, at most there'd be a few sheep. A sheep, Bernard argued, could still certainly be aggressive, but Jim assured him that the only things to watch out for in fields in Scotland were rabbit holes and cowpats. There definitely wouldn't be any animals in this field except a huge number of rabbits, he said, but he couldn't guarantee that they wouldn't be were-rabbits. Besides, the gate had sunk so deep into the ground that it wouldn't even open, so presumably no large animals had come this way any time recently. They'd simply have to climb over it, he finished. Which he then did.

The others stood by the gate helplessly. Rachel was the first to pluck up her courage and climb over as well. Jim held out a hand on the other side and helped her down, and the others watched and decided it was doable. They didn't want to make a fool of themselves though, none of them did. Andrew and David climbed over the gate. The boss and Bernard were visibly put out and had no desire to make laughing stocks of themselves. Luckily it was dark by now. Liz pulled herself together. It couldn't be that bad. She was wearing brand-new walking boots at least, bought specially for this trip, she was sure you could climb in them too, and why else had she been doing Pilates for years? She stepped onto the lower rung of the gate, swung her other leg over, and didn't know which way round and exactly where to put her foot on the other side. To have both feet pointing inwards seemed far too inelegant even in the dark and, besides, she was scared of twisting her knee. She slipped and landed painfully with her thigh against the gate. She swore softly. Jim advised her to place her foot the other way around. She had to admit that he was right but doing so tasted bitter. Luckily, Andrew at least had already gone on ahead, apparently hoping for a phone signal somewhere out here. At any rate, he was staring at his phone, as usual. The blue light illuminated his face. David too had discreetly turned away after noticing how clumsy she was being and was looking at the surroundings. Well thank you very much, this was all equally humiliating! Actually, David didn't care how his boss got over the gate, he was genuinely enjoying the sight of the dark landscape. It had been grey and brown by daylight too, but he liked the emptiness and the quiet which seemed to lie upon everything, and he imagined how beautiful it must be when the heather bloomed or in summer when the woods were green. He heard the cry of a bird of prey, a sheep was bleating somewhere, and in front of him rabbits fled before Mervyn, who had crept beneath the gate. To the north you could just make out the Highlands, to the south you could see down into the valley. A few human dwellings were scattered far apart from one another, their windows lit up. He could only hear the sounds of the woods. And of his colleagues, who just now were silent.

Jim held out his hand to Liz, who reluctantly let him help her. His hand was warm and rough and strong. Her reluctance vanished. She could have held onto that hand for longer – but she banished this thought immediately. Bernard was the last to climb clumsily over the gate, nobody helping him because he wouldn't have let himself be helped anyway. Even Jim and Liz turned away, they all went on a few steps and left Bernard to face this challenge alone. Which was just fine by him. He was a banker, and a banker's not a monkey, after all. Luckily, the gate on the other side of the field was easier to open, and so they headed home without further incident, although not necessarily in the best of spirits.

Liz wanted to get under a hot shower before she did anything else. The long journey, her outbreaks of sweat after those terror-inducing bird attacks, then the walk in the cold – a shower would do her good, she thought, and the Lady had specifically mentioned the new shower unit. Normally the cold didn't bother her at all, she'd rather be cold than hot, she loved winter. But right now she was freezing.

Beneath the shower though, she couldn't help but swiftly realise that while the water was admittedly lovely and warm, it dripped out of the showerhead so weakly that it didn't even reach most of her wet body. She was still freezing in the shower, so hurried instead of taking her time and enjoying it and was done before she would have liked. She should have chosen the room with the bathtub for the ladies after all, she would have loved a hot bath right now. And that way she could have been alone for a while too. The men were all peculiar in their own ways and weren't always easy to put up with. She rubbed herself dry, pulled on all the warm things she had with her and let the cook pour her a cup of tea. Then she sat herself in front of the fire, which the cook had kept going in the sitting room, and slowly warmed up again. At least a little. None of this was going at all how she'd imagined it. She had wanted a bit of seclusion so the men wouldn't constantly be goofing about online and could all concentrate properly, but it really didn't need to be quite this isolated, Andrew was right about that. And she still wasn't sure whether this shrink had been such a good idea. The head of the board of directors had urgently recommended some kind of teambuilding measures to her because tensions simply kept surfacing in her department, and in the end she had agreed because it occurred to her that her old uni friend offered just such a thing. And now he had sent his colleague instead, who seemed perfectly nice, but – *personal catalogue on feedback culture*, for goodness sake! They had been working together for years, they were grownups, they really didn't need to bother with that kind of thing any more. Somehow she had imagined it differently, with a more concrete focus on their work. Instead they had to draw boats as if they were at nursery. She might have to have a little talk with Rachel.

The atmosphere at dinner was polite. What Helen had described as *just a bite* turned out to be a feast. She had been clever with her advance planning, bringing two kinds of homemade coleslaw with her, and she had made three very different but equally delicious salads while the group were drawing ships and going on walks. She had heated up the soup and arranged cheese and cold cuts and crackers prettily on plates, and the bankers were all most pleasantly surprised by what she had referred to as *nothing special* and found themselves looking forward to the following days. At least to the food. When the group had returned to the house, Jim and David had walked on a bit further with Mervyn, while Andrew and Bernard had withdrawn to their rooms. The boss had showered, while Rachel had given Helen a hand and set the table. Having a bit of time more or less to themselves had done the bankers good, and so while they were still noncommittal and distant with each other, they at least appeared somewhat more relaxed. It seemed to Rachel as if the bankers didn't know each other at all. You wouldn't have thought they had been working together for years.

Which was why it was even more important to hold the session on feedback culture after dinner, she thought, so that they could really get stuck in tomorrow morning. One or two of them were having a drink with the meal – Jim had a beer, Andrew a cider, David a red wine. In general, she realised that everyone was drinking something different. The boss was drinking tea, Bernard Irn-Bru. When in Scotland, he said, you have to drink Irn-Bru. At home he tended to drink coke, Irn-Bru was too sweet. The others thought Irn-Bru too sweet for anyone over the age of twelve, but Bernard's culinary tastes weren't particularly refined. Really, Rachel would have rather liked a glass of white wine, but she hadn't quite dared to ask for yet another different drink. Besides, she wanted to keep a clear head for the evening session and so she stuck to tea.

After dinner, Jim stoked the fire in the sitting room, Andrew helped Helen to clear the table, David withdrew to his room for a bit, and Bernard went to take a bath. The men had already planned their different bath times so that there would always be enough time in between for the water to heat up again. They started with the feedback session before Bernard was back. Bernard took his time, he considered this whole business with the feedback catalogue unnecessary anyway. Without anyone asking her to, the cook brought gin and tonics into the sitting room for everyone, and she made sure that Bernard got one too as soon as he came out of the bathroom. She was a clever woman, the cook.

While drawing up their personal catalogue on feedback culture, they were thus all drinking the same thing, although they all had different bags of crisps. Everyone but the boss, that is. Her stupid hormones were bothering her in more ways than one. The alcohol and the log fire were having their effect – the bankers just wanted to get this over with now and said all the things you're supposed to say in these situations. They wanted to always make their feedback about the situation and never the individual, they wanted to always remember that the recipient of their feedback was a person too, they wanted to use I-statements, they never wanted to move from talking about the thing to talking about the individual, and so on. Andrew rolled his eyes, and when Rachel signalled that they had enough and declared the session over, he told the others that he'd take the dog out for a moment. Actually, he had realised on the way back from the walk that there was a spot behind the house where he could access the McIntoshes' wifi with his phone. When he got the chance, he'd have to ask them whether it was okay for him to use their internet. The network wasn't secured with a password, so he assumed it was intended to be used. He didn't want to browse for long anyway, only to wish his wife good night. He couldn't just go to sleep without at least sending her an email and seeing whether she had written to him. It was the least he could do if he couldn't call her, which is what they normally did when one or the other of them was travelling. It was really beautiful here, he wrote, romantic … not exactly luxurious though and freezing cold. He didn't have any phone signal, the food was excellent, the cook an absolute marvel, the atmosphere was otherwise business-like. They had had to draw boats. Bernard was annoying him, he'd far rather be here with her and the children. She should give his love to the children, and he hoped she'd sleep well.

She had written to him too. She had tried to call him, she said, but clearly he had no signal or had turned his phone off. She hoped that he had arrived okay, that everything was going well and he could at least get online. She was already looking forward to his return. His daughter had won a bronze medal in gymnastics at sports club and was very proud.

On the way back to the house, he trod in some goose muck. Mervyn had fetched the toy monkey and wanted to play. Andrew was already very fond of Mervyn, but the stuffed monkey really was revolting, the boss was right about that. And he could have done without the goose muck. But not without wishing his wife a good night.

There were only a few sentences of conversation to be heard in the shared rooms once they were all in bed. Bernard and David disagreed about the necessity of unpacking their suitcases. In other words: David thought they might as well leave their things in their cases, they were only here for three nights after all, while Bernard had tidied everything neatly into the wardrobe. They didn't have any further topics of conversation. David read a little, Bernard fell asleep immediately. Jim and Andrew chatted about ice houses and Douglas Adams but carefully avoided anything to do with the bank. They too soon fell asleep.

Rachel and Helen, meanwhile, both felt they had found an ally. Neither of them was part of the group and they were glad of it. Both sensed that the other had a similar view of things but they didn't talk about it, for they didn't yet know each other well enough. They were sleeping in the same bed, that was enough intimacy for the first night. But they had certainly exchanged the odd look now and again during the day, and Rachel in particular was very glad not to be alone with these strange banker people.

Lord McIntosh was an early riser. Stepping out of the house at the crack of dawn the next morning, he heard it right away: the by now familiar sound of a peacock's beak on car paint. He ran up to the investment department manager's car, chased the peacock away (an activity he was now fairly practiced at) and inspected the damage. A few dents and scratches and some chipped paint on the left wing, near the boot. The curtains in the west wing were shut, the guests were evidently still asleep and probably hadn't seen or heard anything. They would be staying a few more days and were as important as they were difficult. It couldn't go on like this. Hamish was hopeful more wealthy bankers would follow if they heard this group had enjoyed their stay, so he wanted to make sure that they did. Neither he nor Ryszard could spend whole days at a time keeping the peacock away, and it was too late to ask the investment department manager to put her car in the garage – which he would have had to clear out first anyway – because then he would have to admit to and explain the damage which had already occurred, and that just wasn't an option. The impression he'd had of the lady so far was enough to prevent him from even considering it. Look at how she'd reacted to a wee bit of goose muck on her shoe! It was clearly best for her to know nothing about the damage – and for him to be ignorant of it too. Without further ado, the Laird fetched Britney and Albert from the kitchen and his gun from the cupboard, picked up the bucket of feed and tried to lure the crazy peacock into the woods. He could hardly shoot it right in front of the house – that would be sure to wake the guests, and then he'd be forced to explain himself. If they heard a distant shot from the woods, it could always be put down to the shooting season. After all, the sound of shots wasn't all that unusual at this time of year. The peacock, however, continued to eye up the blue car and wasn't nearly as interested in the bucket of feed as the Laird had hoped. Britney was jumping around barking hysterically and didn't understand anything, and even Albert took a while to understand that he was meant to make sure the peacock came with them. It had been made extremely clear to him that he was to leave the peacocks alone. Yesterday all of the peacocks had been taken into the woods, and he'd understood that – herding was what he did. But he wasn't normally allowed to have anything to do with a peacock on its own and besides, a peacock wasn't exactly a sheep. All the while, Britney was yapping so much that she must surely have woken the first of the bankers, the peacock was screaming, and the Laird was trying to make it clear to Albert what he wanted him to do, the whole time squinting at the windows of the west wing and hoping none of the curtains would be drawn aside. But eventually Albert did what was expected of him. The Laird went ahead with the bucket of feed.

Albert drove the peacock a little way into the woods. At first they went along the path, but then the Laird left the path and Albert struggled to keep the peacock under control, for it was evidently irritated by the barking in particular and by Albert and Britney in general, and fled into the trees. At some point it had had enough of the game and just stayed put, perched on the lower branches of an oak. Hamish told Albert that'd do, he could go and play and stop barking. Which Albert did, taking Britney with him.

The Laird meanwhile stood next to the tree where the peacock was perched and looked up at the bird. He had to do what he had to do. But it wasn't pleasant.

The deed now done, it occurred to the Laird that he couldn't exactly return to the house with a gun in one hand and a dead peacock in the other. It had taken a while to lure the peacock so far into the woods and, well, perhaps he had put off shooting it for a wee while too. The first bankers were sure to be awake by now and might not appreciate the sight of a dead peacock at breakfast. And he couldn't have explained the situation without mentioning the damage to the manager's car. So he left the peacock lying where it was, somewhere in the undergrowth, and covered it with some leaves and a few sticks so that it wasn't immediately obvious from the path. He hid the gun under a pile of stones nearby and went back to the house. He wasn't exactly whistling cheerfully – it really was such a shame about the lovely peacock, but you had to know when enough was enough. And before the next person to come along was an old lady with a blue rinse and the peacock pecked her head open, he'd rather err on the side of caution. He wasn't going to be sentimental. The peacock had been dangerous, Hamish hadn't had a choice. And he hadn't been particularly attached to the creature. After all, a peacock wasn't exactly a dog.

Mervyn, however, most certainly was a dog. The group went on a short morning walk before breakfast. Mervyn needed to be walked, and Helen didn't have breakfast ready yet because the boss had taken so long in the bathroom. It was Andrew's turn for the men's bathroom, but he would have to wait until after breakfast, as the other three had taken their turns before him. Needing to save water, the first three had only been in for a lick and a promise. They weren't used to having to queue for the bathroom or to finding the dregs of their predecessor's toothpaste in the sink, they hadn't had their breakfasts yet, and they were in accordingly bad moods. The boss hadn't fared particularly well in the bathroom either. She hadn't showered at all, as it would have been freezing again, so she'd just washed standing up instead. It was freezing. She'd even fetched one of the fan heaters into the bathroom for a bit to at least warm up the air a little, but with only moderately satisfactory results. Once she'd washed, she got dressed quickly before taking her time to do her makeup and hair. Bernard was in a particularly bad mood. He had slept surprisingly well, but the first thing he discovered upon waking was that it isn't particularly easy to get down from an upper bunk, and it hadn't escaped him that David had needed to stifle a laugh. Eventually he had somehow managed to clamber down with a fair amount of banging and crashing. At one point he almost fell, which was particularly embarrassing in front of David, who was ten years his junior.

Mervyn was the only member of the party who was genuinely looking forward to the day and to the walk. He jumped around, ran ahead for a bit and then ran back and was generally excited to be alive, while the humans remained silent or only spoke to each other when necessary. Mervyn found the somewhat older man the most agreeable. He was always friendly really. Him and the woman who was always in the kitchen and who sometimes slipped Mervyn things to eat. Meanwhile, his mistress, for some reason, didn't react enthusiastically at all when he brought her the soft toy which smelt of the other dog. Liz still thought the monkey repulsive and ordered Mervyn to drop it. Mervyn didn't understand why, but he obeyed and was soon happy again. There was plenty else to discover: the old ice house and the half-ruined chapel, which the humans didn't even notice because it was behind a hedge and concealed by trees, and the humans always stuck to the paths.

Mervyn roamed through the undergrowth the way dogs do. Leaving the humans behind for a bit, he followed his nose and found a dead peacock. He was puzzled for a moment, as he hadn't noticed that this was a shooting party and he hadn't heard any shots, but he could smell it clearly – and a shot bird which was still warm must of course be retrieved. The setter knew his duties. And so he carried the peacock back to his mistress. It was only a tiny bit ruffled and Mervyn was satisfied and proud, wagging his tail and looking forward to being praised and patted.

He didn't understand at all why instead she shouted at him and told him off, even hit him, which she never normally did, and why there was suddenly this unpleasant commotion amongst the humans. They were all quite beside themselves but clearly not with joy. They were angry with him. He drew in his tail and crept away. He had done everything just right!

The investment department deliberated on what to do. Jim was in favour of confessing to the McIntoshes. He felt sure that they would understand a dog killing a peacock, they were clearly fond of dogs, after all. And they could buy them a new peacock – maybe some kind of insurance would even cover it. Under absolutely no circumstances, the boss told the department, they didn't know what kind of relationship the McIntoshes had with their peacocks, they were clearly even fond of that aggressive goose. It might turn out they were as attached to the peacock as they were to their dog, and where would that land her and Mervyn? No, that wasn't an option. The dead peacock had to go.

What did she mean, go? asked David.

Well, he was to get rid of it, said the boss, who was always being told she was a control freak and now wanted to prove that she most certainly was capable of delegating. What does she mean, get rid of it? thought David, but out loud he said, alright, he'd deal with it. They weren't here to have fun after all, and the boss was the boss. In the meantime, they hid the dead peacock under some foliage, but the boss was of the opinion that this wasn't a good enough hiding place. The McIntoshes' dog would ferret the peacock out of there in the end and then it'd all come out. David was to think of something and make the peacock disappear. Her tone made it clear that no argument would be brooked. They returned to the house in gloomy spirits. Mervyn crept along behind them with his tail tucked between his legs. He still didn't understand what he'd done wrong.

Lord Hamish McIntosh sat in the kitchen and stirred his tea. Such a shame about the lovely peacock! But what else could he have done? Mating season had been over ages ago and the peacock had clearly remained crazy for good. He had been a safety risk, it was probably pure luck that the bird had only ever attacked objects. No one wants to mess with an aggressive peacock.

Like him, his wife would regret it but take it in her stride. She was very pragmatic when it came to this sort of thing. But it would hit Aileen hard. She was fond of every single animal. When she was cleaning, she even caught spiders and carried them outside, rather than just hoovering them up with Henry or stamping on them, as anyone else would have done, and she insisted on catching mice with humane traps and releasing them elsewhere. The Laird decided not to tell Aileen he'd shot the peacock. She probably had as little clue as anyone else how many peacocks lived on the estate. Ryszard, however, had to be told, because then he could return his attention to more important tasks than luring the whole gaggle of peacocks into the woods three times a day. Hamish would then also have to ask Ryszard not to mention it to Aileen either. Hamish hated this kind of thing, it seemed so dishonest. But Aileen's usual cheerful nature – dented when she'd broken her arm – was only just returning, and he didn't need to now burden her with the fact that he'd shot a peacock. How would he be able to look her in the eye?

Unfortunately, the first person to come into the kitchen was Aileen. And, of course, she noticed straight away that something wasn't quite right. But when he didn't come out with whatever it was despite her asking, she didn't probe any further – she was far too well brought up for that. The Laird was still the Laird and it probably wasn't any of her business. Remarkable enough that she was sitting in his kitchen eating breakfast with him. Really, she should have made his breakfast, but she was hampered by her arm and so instead he was pretty much making hers. He made her tea, and while she could put the toaster on herself, he had to spread the butter for her. The Laird was a kind man. But something was bothering him. When Lady Fiona joined them, he quickly took his leave and left for the university, where he taught Greek and Latin. He wanted to drive by Ryszard's first and discuss the jobs that needed doing that day. Aileen was almost a little jealous, she would have liked to have dropped by Ryszard's too and have him spread her next piece of toast. Greek and Latin, however, she considered superfluous – she just didn't see the point in them nowadays.

Aileen didn't notice anything unusual about Lady Fiona. And indeed, there wasn't anything unusual about Lady Fiona. After all, she didn't yet know that the Laird had shot the peacock.

David had a problem. He felt sick. He hardly ate any breakfast, just nibbled at a piece of toast, drank his tea and brooded. He didn't want to touch the dead peacock, neither with his bare hands nor with his peccary leather gloves, and he had absolutely no idea how he was meant to get rid of it. A peacock isn't exactly a blackbird, it's pretty big. His only option was probably to carry it deeper into the woods and bury it – but what with? The ground might already be frozen and much too hard to dig a grave, and anyway he didn't have a spade and could hardly dig with his hands. On top of all that, how was he meant to explain himself if someone caught him? And just how was he meant to take the peacock deeper into the woods without touching it? He was quite distraught. After breakfast, he just stayed put in the kitchen. Helen had noticed over breakfast that David, who seemed to be fairly reserved by nature anyway, was quieter than he had been the night before and even looked quite pale. Something was bothering him, and the cook – with all her maternal ways – was always happy to offer comfort, with cakes and biscuits and stew.

But David didn't want any cake or any maternal comfort. He wanted a whisky. At this time of the morning. And he got one. It was perfectly clear to Helen that he didn't have a drink problem but rather that something must have happened on the morning walk. The rest of the bankers had seemed even more tense than they had the night before too.

David asked for another whisky. Helen raised an eyebrow. After the third whisky he explained his problem. There was a dead peacock in the woods, killed by the boss's Irish setter. And now he was meant to dispose of it. And he had no idea how. And his boss most certainly would not be amused if he didn't succeed – and you knew what that meant, if Helen didn't mind him saying so. The cook put this down to the alcohol, surely the young man wouldn't have otherwise been so blunt. You couldn't just hide a peacock like that, said David, it had to be buried. And was he meant to break into the McIntoshes' shed to steal a spade or something? That just wasn't on! What if he got caught when stealing the spade? Or when burying the peacock? How was he meant to explain that to the Laird and Lady? He wasn't a thief, he said. And he wasn't a lumberjack or an undertaker either. He was a banker.

Then he drank another whisky.

The cook thought about it for a split second.

And I, she said quietly, I am a cook.

Aileen had realised there was one thing she could do wonderfully despite her arm being in plaster, and that was to take the dogs for a walk. Normally they'd just roam around alone outside, but Albert, who had always tended to extend his wanderings just that bit too far, had been doing so more than ever since Victoria's death. The McIntoshes kept having to drive down the road and ask the various far-flung neighbours whether they'd seen him. In summer he could often be found by following the smell of barbecue, or a neighbour might pick him up somewhere out and about and bring him home. It was harder in the winter, people didn't go out as much. So the McIntoshes were quite happy when Aileen went on long walks with Albert and Britney and made sure that Albert came home afterwards. Albert seemed to value Britney's being there anyway – no wonder, he'd spent almost all his life with Victoria and clearly didn't like being alone. Just like the goose. The McIntoshes had already talked about needing to get a second dog. They kept thinking that they really had enough animals now and agreeing not to acquire any more, but then they kept finding new reasons to change their minds. They had enough space, the dogs had a wonderful life and it was so painful to see how lonely Albert was. The goose's loneliness was bad enough – but in her case, they had decided to stay tough.

A few years ago, they had renovated the entire first floor and had installed a pale brown carpet, because they'd had a long-haired, light brown collie mongrel at the time. The dog had shed so much hair on their dark blue sofa, making it look so dreadful, that for the renovation Fiona had genuinely chosen the carpet to match the dog, so that it wouldn't be quite as obvious that everything was covered in dog hair. They also got a new sofa at this point, and the dog was immediately forbidden from sitting on it. Instead they bought him a basket with a pale brown blanket.

Unfortunately, this very dog had died unexpectedly just six months later. Since then, the McIntoshes had only had light brown dogs, and Fiona always insisted that she wouldn't take in a black or a white dog ever again. She had installed the carpet to match the dog once – from now on any dogs coming into the house were to match the carpet. The Laird and Aileen were never quite sure how seriously she meant this. If a black dog in need of a home had stood at the door and looked up at her with big round eyes, then of course she'd have taken it in – she wasn't heartless! And in the end, it wasn't like a dog was a lump of rock. To tell the truth, they had never looked for or even bought a dog, they somehow always just ended up with them because the dogs needed a home just when the McIntoshes happened to have space. It was pure coincidence that both Albert and Victoria had matched the colour scheme.

Right now though, it wasn't a black dog in need of a home at the door, just the postie. He said hello to Aileen, Britney and Albert, who were about to leave, asked after Aileen's arm and offered to drive her into the village should she ever need a lift. She could come back on the afternoon school bus. Aileen thanked him for the offer, wrapped a scarf around her neck and let Lady Fiona tie her shoelaces and do up the zip on her jacket. She'd got used to this and it was no longer quite as embarrassing as it had been at first. She had soon recovered her practical and cheerful nature, and she found herself laughing at her own helplessness more and more. Aileen and the dogs hit the road.

The postie handed Lady Fiona the post, which included a letter from the Bakshis. Their car had been repaired ages ago, but there had been a ridiculous back and forth with the insurance, who at first had responded that they only covered damages caused by pets, i.e. by dogs, cats and horses, and that peacocks weren't pets. It had been fairly easy to prove that they were indeed pets, that peacocks were a non-indigenous species and therefore not wildfowl, but then the person responsible had doubted the truth of their story entirely, and the four of them had been required to make a written statement.

The insurance, wrote the Bakshis, had finally paid up, and the story had caused so much mirth among their friends as to make it entirely worth it. So as far as they were concerned, everything was now sorted. They thanked the McIntoshes for dealing with the matter so generously and emphasised once again how at home they'd felt in the valley and how happy they'd be to accept the offer to return. Indeed, they wrote, they'd already wondered about maybe travelling to Scotland for New Year – would the cottages be warm enough? And were they even rented out over the winter? They said they would call sometime in the coming week in order to inquire.

Fiona McIntosh was pleased. She always threw a big party at Hogmanay – all their friends came and played silly games, which ended up with thirty adults squatting under the giant dining table and having a blast. After midnight there was always an impromptu ceilidh. She was sure the Bakshis would fit right in. Such friendly people!

Lady Fiona McIntosh phoned her husband, who must have arrived at the university by now, to tell him the good news. Hamish was pleased, not only that the Bakshis wanted to come for Hogmanay but also that his wife had called, as he had something to tell her too. Albeit something rather more unpleasant. His wife took it in her stride, and as he'd expected, she agreed they'd do better not to say anything to Aileen – she was having a rough enough time of it with her broken arm. Hamish loved his wife very much for wanting to spare Aileen but didn't say so. Fiona loved her husband very much for the same reason, but she didn't say so either.

Aileen decided to knock on the door to the west wing. She explained that her name was Aileen and that normally she was the housekeeper and responsible for the cottages but that she'd broken her arm and couldn't do much at the moment. Except go for walks. She was taking Albert and Britney out and so just wanted to ask whether she should take Mervyn out too. He was called Mervyn, wasn't he? Or Justin?

Jim opened the door and was immediately enchanted. The young woman wasn't wearing anything special, just jeans and some old jacket, and her arm was fully encased in plaster, but she had such a sparkle in her eyes, and she radiated charm. He hadn't understood her first sentence because of her broad Scots accent, so he still didn't know who she was. Once he'd heard his way into the second sentence, he decided the accent was charming too. Just as he was about to introduce himself, Mervyn shot past him and greeted the other dogs ecstatically. Jim told her his name and that he was glad to meet her and then called both his boss and Mervyn, who surely shouldn't be playing around with the other dogs in the woods and potentially killing a second animal. Or perhaps even fetching the dead peacock which he already had on his conscience. Now that he'd had time to think about it, Jim thought the whole thing wasn't like Mervyn at all, but who knew what went through a dog's mind? Having tasted blood once, perhaps he'd lead the other two dogs to join in further acts of idiocy and together they might attack a sheep. You did hear stories like that. It was up to the boss to say something herself.

The boss arrived and said that Mervyn had already been outside that morning, and she wasn't sure that he'd obey Aileen. She didn't want to risk him running away, she said, and it would be best for him to stay here with them but many thanks for the offer. Aileen was baffled by how rude the lady was and didn't understand her concern. What exactly was meant to happen? The setter wouldn't get lost in the company of the other dogs, who knew their way around, and Mervyn was hardly likely to be hit by a car up here either. People from cities really were strange sometimes, and this posh cow seemed to think her dog unusually stupid. But Aileen was polite enough to keep her thoughts to herself. She said goodbye (somewhat more warmly to the lovely older gentleman than to the posh cow) and left with Britney and Albert. Mervyn didn't understand why he wasn't allowed to go with them and whimpered pitifully.

The cook was of a much more practical nature than the easily intimidated David. The first thing she did was take the rubbish out. She had actually spotted the wheelie bins a while ago, but she knocked on the McIntoshes' door nonetheless and politely asked where she should empty the rubbish and whether food waste was collected separately. Drawing Lady Fiona into a conversation, she chatted about how beautiful the region was, and the nature in the valley, and quite naturally moved on to talking about the animals, namely the gorgeous peacocks. The Lady was never averse to a cosy chat – besides, the cook seemed so friendly – and so she readily answered her questions. Helen discovered that no one really knew exactly how many peacocks there were by now, or how many young they'd had this year and how many of those had survived. The creatures were normally to be seen in groups of twos and threes rather than all together, so the exact number could only be guessed at. In fact, Aileen probably did know how many peacocks there were. Aileen loved all animals equally and knew everything anyway – she could even tell the peacocks apart. But Lady Fiona didn't tell the cook that. Although she was worried that sooner or later Aileen would notice there was a peacock missing. Instead she told Helen about the peacocks losing their long tail feathers after the mating season and growing new ones each year, which astounded her every single time. She didn't say that one of the peacocks had gone mad and had attacked anything which was blue – after all, her husband had told her on the phone that the boss's blue car had been damaged. Fiona wanted to take a closer look herself as soon as the group was no longer nearby. Surely they'd go for a walk at some point, then she could take a look at the car without anyone noticing.

Helen was reassured, as she could safely assume no one would notice a peacock was missing. To be honest, she shared Jim's opinion that they ought to confess to the McIntoshes about Mervyn killing the bird, anything else seemed dishonest. But her opinion hadn't been asked, the boss had made a different decision and had expressed herself in no uncertain terms. At least there was a realistic chance they wouldn't be busted. She was also reassured that food waste was just to go into the main bin, which meant she'd be able to hide the bones, feathers and any other remains which were clearly from a peacock under the rest of the rubbish.

Helen also took the opportunity to ask where the nearest shop was – did they really have to drive the twelve miles to the village? She'd brought most of the food they needed with her, she explained, but she'd quite like to buy some fresh vegetables and stuff like that.

What had once been the home farm, of course, also belonged to the McIntoshes' estate. In his spare time, Ryszard grew all sorts of fruit and vegetables there and sold them in his small shop, along with other food items and basic necessities, to holidaymakers and to other folk who lived in the glen. Ryszard was working somewhere in the glen at the moment, Lady Fiona explained, but she'd give Helen the key to the shop, Helen should just fetch what she needed and write it all down. They could pay later, Ryszard would drop by the west wing when he was back. Helen asked the Lady for directions to the farm. Then she commanded David, intimidated and clearly

74

tipsy, to drive her because she didn't know exactly where the dead peacock was.

David feebly protested that he'd already drunk three whiskies – or was it four? – and so wasn't able to drive, but Helen wasn't having any of it. He had expressly been given the task of getting rid of the peacock, she pointed out, and he could hardly tell his boss he'd delegated the job to the cook. Anyway, they were in the middle of nowhere, and everything, even the farm, was on the McIntoshes' property – they probably didn't need to worry about large volumes of traffic or about being pulled over by the police.

And so the capable cook and the drunk banker put on their walking boots and drove into the woods. Shopping, as they told those staying at home, and to make the peacock disappear.

David couldn't believe it. The woman must be mad! She didn't seriously want to bring the peacock into the house and cook it? And make him, David, an accessory to the crime? She couldn't just serve up the peacock – which the boss's dog had killed – to the boss herself, who was as tyrannical as she was hysterical. What did peacock even taste like? What made Helen think you could eat peacocks? How would she know how to cook such a creature?

Was she really sure, he started.

She was so looking forward to it, chirped the cook. Peacock, she exclaimed, it had been an age since she'd last cooked peacock!

David asked whether she really had cooked peacock before.

Helen had indeed worked for a while at a London restaurant known for its unusual dishes, where occasionally, quite rarely, peacock was on the menu. As was ostrich. Personally, she didn't like the taste of ostrich so much, she told him, it had such a strong taste and was so lean as to be chewy. Of course, you could work with that, but it wasn't her personal favourite. Peacock on the other hand! Very tender meat, as long as you cooked it for long enough, a little like pheasant, and you could serve it so beautifully on a large platter, with a tasty filling of dried fruits, for example, and the head laid decoratively beside it. The banker went pale. At festive banquets in the middle ages they served swans and peacocks in their own plumage, Helen went on. The skin was removed in its entirety along with the feathers, and then a wireframe was placed inside to strengthen it, so that an almost lifelike swan or peacock would sit on the table – it must have looked beautiful – and the roast swan or peacock or stew, or whatever had been cooked, would be underneath. There was even some legend about a saint, she said, in which a cooked peacock got up from the table and flew away, but sadly she'd forgotten the details of the story.

Back then, they had to cook the meat for ages, she said, until it fell apart of its own accord, because dentistry care at the time left an awful lot to be desired or, in other words, because most people only had a few rotting stumps left in their mouths and could barely chew. Helen chuckled. David felt sick.

She would have loved to learn how to cook cats and dogs too, Helen continued, but unfortunately that was taboo in England. And yet people wanted to eat crocodiles and ostriches, which didn't even live here! That kind of thing annoyed her. Why did the English want to eat ostrich meat but not dogs?

David took a deep breath. He loved his dog, he loved all dogs, like any sane person. It was the most obvious thing in the world to him that you didn't eat dogs. After all, he didn't eat people, and a dog wasn't exactly a pig.

But why not? asked Helen. It wasn't like a dog was cleverer or cleaner or in any other way more developed than a pig. Though the developmental level was a stupid argument anyway, she said. For example, the fact that fish weren't as complex as other creatures didn't give you the right to torture them. In her opinion, the problem wasn't which animals you ate but rather how you treated them while they were alive. She loved horses, she said, but she still ate them, and she didn't particularly love fish, but she was nevertheless of the opinion that they deserved a decent life. David recognised that she was right, but only on a theoretical level. In practice, he didn't want to think about eating horses or peacocks at all. Really, he just wanted to go back to bed and pull the covers up over his head. But he didn't say that.

One thing they did agree on was that it would be better not to tell the boss they'd be serving her the peacock Mervyn had killed. The boss and the rest of their companions were to believe they'd taken the peacock deeper into the woods and buried it, heaping dead leaves and stones on the grave.

Helen had thought of everything. David had not. She'd realised she couldn't smuggle the whole peacock, feathers and all, into the west wing. Officially though, they weren't just getting rid of the peacock but were also going shopping, so they certainly could return with a bird ready for the pot. Which meant she had to pluck and draw the peacock in the woods. She had brought along a footstool, an apron and a sharp knife, and got to work. She put the dead peacock on her lap. David went pale again. She would now open the carotid artery, remove the bird's head and let it bleed dry, she explained. She did hope the blood hadn't clotted too much, you really ought to do this directly after the animal's death so the blood would run out nicely. In fact, she added, it was best when the heart was still beating and pumped the blood out. Well, this would have to do. Perhaps in the meantime David would like to go for a short walk, she suggested, and find a place where they could bury the feathers and the entrails. She'd need a good half hour to pluck and draw the peacock. He'd surely be able to find somewhere suitable in that time.

David gratefully took her up on the suggestion. He only managed a few steps before he threw up, just as the cook removed the peacock's head and the first torrent of blood streamed out. David had already turned his back. By the time the peacock was bled dry, he had lost not only his breakfast but the four whiskies too.

Helen reflected that young city folk nowadays couldn't cope with anything, but she kept this recognition to herself. Somehow, she liked the poor guy. There was a bottle of water in the car, she called after him. David hurried away.

By the time he returned a good half hour later, he looked a lot better and most of Helen's work was done. The prudent cook had put the bird, now plucked and drawn, in a big plastic bag. It no longer looked like a peacock, merely like a lump of meat – despite the fact that it still had the finest of its feathers. The next time the group went out for a walk, she'd have to scorch these off over the gas stove and hope to get the smell out of the kitchen before anyone grew suspicious. Ideally, she'd fry some onions and garlic at the same time and cook an aromatic soup. She had gathered the plucked feathers into a second bag as best she could, and the entrails had gone in there too. The only exception was the liver, for which she'd brought a Tupperware. She was planning to make a lovely liver pâté.

She asked David whether he was alright.

Yes, thanks, he was feeling better, he told her and apologised.

They took a while to decide what to do with the feathers. Luckily, it wasn't mating season and the peacock didn't have any long tail feathers any more, but even so, they were pretty long and there were plenty of them. Of course, there were peacock feathers lying around all over the estate, as it wasn't unusual for the birds to shed a few. But never so many at once. In the end they stuffed most of them, along with the entrails, the head and the feet (David turned pale yet again), under a pile of leaves. Helen wasn't afraid of picking up the raw entrails, and David was able to limit himself to collecting sticks and stones and piling these up like a grave mound over the remains of the peacock. He could hardly think about the severed head and feet without feeling sick again. They hoped the remains would all decompose before anyone found them, but chances were no one would go so deep into the woods and clear away the sticks and stones anyway. At most a dog. They decided to simply take some of the longer tail feathers with them and claim that they'd gathered them as a present for Helen's little nieces. Helen found the whole thing mightily amusing. David tried to see the humour in it too but didn't quite manage.

Next they went to Ryszard's farm shop to buy vegetables. They opened up the shop and picked up tomatoes, onions, carrots, courgettes, red cabbage, brussels sprouts and fresh herbs. The cook was impressed at the range which this man – who seemed more like an old soldier than anything else – had on offer in Scotland in November. Behind the farmhouse, Ryszard had a greenhouse and a small ice house. The ice house was inset into an earth wall and built with stone, and he stored potatoes, carrots and apples there, as well as anything else for which the conditions were suitable. He must take as much pleasure from fresh vegetables as she did, Helen thought. She and David weighed everything and listed the amounts in the book provided for this purpose.

On the way home, Helen raved about the idea of roasting the peacock whole, stuffed with raisins, prunes and dried apricots and wrapped in strips of bacon. Peacock meat could otherwise be a bit too dry, she explained. Or perhaps with a roast dough stuffing which would bake inside the bird as it cooked, she'd like to try that sometime. The banker was impressed, the cook clearly did know her stuff when it came to cooking peacocks. Unfortunately though, the cook added, she wouldn't be able to cook the bird whole, because then she'd have some explaining to do. The peacock really was too big for them to be able to pretend it was a pheasant. And that was her plan, as pheasant meat came closest to peacock in taste. Because of this, she told David, she had decided to cook a curry. Not only would the spice mix change the meat's colour, but the intense flavour would hopefully mask its unusual taste. She chattered so enthusiastically about different ways of cooking peacock that David slowly relaxed and was even beginning to look forward to the peacock curry. And it was somehow a little bit exciting too, going behind the boss's back and serving her peacock without her knowledge.

David had no way of knowing that the main reason the cook was chattering away this much wasn't excited anticipation. Instead it was to cover up her own uncertainty. She had made an astonishing discovery when plucking the peacock: Mervyn hadn't killed the bird after all. That in itself didn't particularly surprise her, for as far as she could see, Mervyn was the most peaceful and obedient dog in the world – or in other words, she thought that, like all Irish setters, he was a little stupid. No, the peacock had been shot. With lead. And this had happened just this morning, for the bird had still been warm and supple, and the blood which poured out had still been fresh. The dog had probably found the dead peacock in the woods and retrieved it, for she had heard he was a trained gun dog and went on shoots with the boss. The peacock must still have smelt of lead.

Her first impulse was to tell the young banker and then tell the investment department manager. The team's boss would surely be relieved to know that her dog was innocent, and the boss being relieved would be good for everyone. The problem was that then she'd have to explain how she had noticed the shot or, more to the point – why she had been plucking the peacock. You wouldn't have spotted the shot holes on the unplucked peacock, as the feathers had shifted back and covered them up. Of course, she could have claimed she had noticed them by chance when helping David to bury the peacock – but what if the manager was sceptical and wanted to see for herself? The manager of the London private bank's investment department would see that half of the peacock had been plucked and would rightly conclude that they had been planning to serve it to her without her knowledge. She wasn't stupid, after all. Helen had only been hired for the weekend, so she didn't need to worry too much about the woman's wrath – other than that she might badmouth her to other potential clients – but David would probably be given the boot, and she could hardly do that to the man. He might have a family, he was in his mid-thirties at most and so at the age where he might have small children, she didn't want to drag him into this. It all sparked new questions though and might prompt new problems. Somebody who was pretty definitely not part of their group knew there was a dead peacock in the woods. Who had shot the peacock and why? And above all: why had they left it in the woods? Would they come back to fetch it? If they'd been planning to just leave it there to decompose, then there wouldn't be a problem. But then why would they have shot it? Surely only to eat it? When whoever it was came back to fetch the peacock, all they'd find would be a few feathers. Would they suspect the group from London of stealing the dead bird? Probably not. Whoever had shot it presumably had something to hide themselves and so would keep quiet. They'd probably been disturbed while poaching.

All this was going through Helen's head as she chatted on about the fact that you could also cook peacock breast fillets very nicely with lemon and basil and serve them with jasmine rice, or bake the drumsticks with apples, cloves and cinnamon and serve them with couscous. David's mouth was beginning to water. And she hadn't even started on the peacock liver pâté.

The cook explained to David once again that peacocks belong to the same family as pheasants and that they'd claim that the meat was pheasant meat. They'd have to make absolutely sure nobody else looked in the larder, she said. The peacock was relatively small but still far too big to be a pheasant. They'd just have to hope, she continued, that his colleagues wouldn't know exactly how big a pheasant was. David said that the boss went shooting, she'd certainly know. Helen hoped keeping Liz out of the larder wouldn't be a problem. After all, she'd hired Helen herself so as to not, under any circumstances, have to go in the kitchen.

But everyone would know that a single pheasant would never be enough for so many people, she continued, so they'd have to claim they'd bought at least two pheasants. But there was only one bird there. At any rate it'd be best if they said as little as possible about the whole thing – and nobody was to look in the larder. It was a bit of a shame they weren't here for longer, the cook added, it'd do the peacock so much good to hang for a few days. And she would have liked to tell everyone what they were eating, instead of palming something so special off as dreary pheasant with nobody knowing what it really was. But there was nothing to be done.

So: officially there would be pheasant curry. If asked, they would tell David's colleagues that Helen had chatted to the Lady to distract her so that David could borrow a spade from the shed without being seen. Then they had buried the dead peacock in the woods and had used the same tactic to return the spade. They hoped, however, that the team wouldn't ask in the first place and that they could just stay quiet rather than having to lie too much. But at least they were agreed upon the official version.

Unofficially, they were both getting more and more of a kick out of the whole affair. They might not have much else in common, but the prospect of deceiving the boss appealed to them both in equal measure. Even if David was still feeling a bit queasy – in mind as well as body. They just hoped the others would already be absorbed in their work and thinking about something else entirely.

In the west wing, the psychologist was explaining the day's task to the others – all except Andrew, who was still in the bathroom. During their stay they were going to perform a number of activities together, so as to gain an awareness of which role each person in the group tended to occupy, she told them. Afterwards they would reflect on what this distribution of roles meant for their work together at the bank – what was good and what was less good, how they could improve the less good and optimise the good. Most of the tasks planned for the next few days would be taking place outdoors; some of the activities would almost be a bit athletic and they'd have to get their hands dirty. Today they were going to be building a den in the woods, so they might want to first of all make sure they were dressed appropriately. This last point was directed at Bernard, who was wearing a suit again.

When Helen and David returned, the boss merely asked whether the peacock had thoroughly disappeared. Very thoroughly, said the cook. David nodded silently. Bernard and Jim were busy putting together some provisions to take with them, a task Helen promptly took off their hands. Rachel explained the plan for the day to David and asked Helen whether it was alright to just take a packed lunch with them – that way they could stay in the woods the whole day. They'd be back for dinner though. This suited the cook very well indeed, as it meant she'd be able to prepare the peacock in peace. Helen was, however, less enthusiastic about the fact that the men had got to work in her kitchen. She'd have to make sure that didn't happen again! She packed sandwiches and fruit, tomatoes and cucumber, olives, a few sausages, some cheese and some chocolate bars – that'd see the bankers through the day, she thought. The boss laughed when she saw the mountains of food packed neatly into bags which had suddenly appeared, as if by magic, on the kitchen table, and asked who on earth was meant to eat all that. Oh, said Helen, with a sideways glance at Jim.

Helen's immediate impression of this business with the den was that it was layman's psychology and unnecessary nonsense; she could already have said who played what role in this group, she didn't need to watch the bankers playing in the woods to do that. Given that these people were all fairly smart, they probably even had a good idea of the relationships themselves. All you had to do was look at them. Jim had picked up something to snack on yet again. You could bet on it that he would have fun building a den and wouldn't be bothered at all about the psychological framework behind it. Bernard's bad mood was, as usual, written all over his face. And Andrew, as ever, looked sceptical. Meanwhile, the boss seemed full of nervous energy on the one hand and contempt for the den-building plan on the other. The cook had already noticed that the boss enjoyed being outdoors but without getting herself dirty, thank you very much. She asked herself how that worked at a shoot. Maybe she had someone to do the dirty work for her.

She didn't doubt that being outside and building a den would absolutely do the bankers good on a number of levels, and the fact that they'd have to get their hands dirty filled her with a sort of mischievous glee. However, she assumed the positive effects of physical activity outside in the fresh air would be counteracted by the fact that it'd all take place under the watchful eyes of the facilitator and their boss. It'd simply be impossible for the men to act naturally under those circumstances. Besides, she wasn't sure building a den was necessarily something you needed to do with your boss and your colleagues, but nobody had asked for her opinion and that was a good thing. Under other circumstances, Helen would have loved to join in building a den, but in this case she was jolly glad that she could just be left in peace to get on with cooking and to scorch off the last of the peacock's downy feathers.

Except that she couldn't. Andrew, who was only just out of the bathroom, refused point blank to take part in this rot, as he called it. He described the task set by the facilitator as a vulgar psychological farce to which he wasn't going to submit. Of course, he said, he was perfectly happy to work with the others developing policies, to discuss their working processes and the division of labour and to critically examine his own role in the team too, but he wasn't going to let himself be forced into self-exposure by his employer. All these children's games were just far too ridiculous. There was nothing that couldn't simply be solved by discussion, and if he wanted to build dens then he'd do so with his children but not with a psychologist and his boss watching – end of story! The man was considerably less cool than he'd have liked to be, Helen could tell he was shaking internally.

Surprisingly, Rachel on the other hand reacted more coolly than she would have trusted herself to. She asked him to reconsider whether it might not be sensible to join in for the sake of the group. This wasn't about exposing him in any way, she said, and she had no interest in voyeurism. She just wanted to help make certain structures visible, but of course it was his decision, and she didn't want to force him to do anything. She sounded a little annoyed, thought Helen, but remarkably she didn't seem particularly offended.

The boss, in contrast, was simmering with rage and would have been very happy to force Andrew to join in. She wasn't here to have fun, after all, and in all honesty, she detested games like this herself, but she had booked the teambuilding and now she wanted it to be a success. She too would rather be sitting in an elegant bar, wearing an Alexander McQueen suit and drinking a well-mixed gin and tonic, not tramping around the woods in a waxed jacket and lined boots. It was one thing for a shoot but quite another when building a den with your colleagues. Secretly she was almost jealous of Andrew for simply refusing to take part, but she couldn't copy him now. The things she did for the corporate climate!

David was keeping a low profile. The outrageous secret he now shared with Helen was enough for him; beyond that, he'd try to remain inconspicuous, as was his nature. Besides, he still wasn't feeling quite a hundred percent after that business with the whisky, and he wasn't in the mood to rebel against anything.

Bernard was a suck-up. Yes, he was discontent, and he most definitely was not excited at the prospect of building a den outside in the woods – not in this cold and certainly not with his colleagues – but he would do whatever the boss suggested. And Jim was satisfied no matter what. So he was going to build a den – well then, that might be quite fun.

Helen could see all of this and thought she could have saved everyone time by just explaining to the psychologist how each person ticked, but she kept this to herself. Besides, Rachel wasn't born yesterday, surely she could see it herself. Who knew, perhaps building a den would prompt unexpected insights after all, sometimes psychologists really could surprise you. And in the end, it wasn't any of her business – she was here to cook. She had her work and Rachel had her own.

Unfortunately, this Andrew character was now sitting in her kitchen making small talk when what she really wanted to do was finish plucking the peacock, scorch off the downy feathers and pick out the lead shot. Instead, she decoratively arranged the peacock feathers allegedly gathered in the woods in a vase. She had hidden the bird itself at the bottom of a crate of vegetables after they'd been to Ryszard's farm shop. David had helped her carry the crate into the kitchen, and she'd immediately hung it up in the larder. The peacock, that is. Nobody had seen it yet and if she had anything to do with it, nobody was going to. To be on the safe side she'd draped a tea towel in such a way as to partially cover the peacock.

When she was done arranging the feathers in the vase, she began to wash up the breakfast things and hoped that sometime soon, some very important matter would occur to Andrew which he would have to go and deal with. The gentleman clearly enjoyed excusing himself from company. Instead, he picked up a tea towel without seeming to think twice about it. Which delighted her on one level but didn't exactly solve her problem.

Liz, David, Jim and Bernard started by looking for a suitable place in the woods to build a den. They didn't really know themselves what they'd consider suitable, they just hoped a spot would catch their eye. David, of course, knew where the remains of the peacock were buried and tried to steer the others as far as possible in a different direction without making it too obvious. He wasn't quite as successful as he would have liked, he felt they were still too close for comfort. He briefly toyed with the idea of telling the others where the body was stashed so they wouldn't remove sticks or stones from the mound by mistake, as they certainly wouldn't want to find the corpse again; but then he thought it better for the others to not even have a clue where the creature – or what remained of it – was interred. Most of the dead peacock lay right at the bottom of the crate of vegetables, after all, and he fervently hoped no one other than Helen would look in the crate. Or that the bird was already hanging in the larder and no longer looked like a peacock. He also hoped Mervyn wouldn't decide to start digging – but ever since the peacock affair, the dog had been on a lead the whole time anyway.

Eventually they found a stack of chopped wood which Jim suggested they could use as one of the walls, that way they'd only need to build three. Or even just two – the final wall could remain open, he said, as a door. The rules Rachel had set were as follows: they could only use materials they found in the woods and which belonged there, so no planks of wood which happened to be lying around and no lost tarpaulins or bits of rubbish. You didn't get many hikers or picnickers here though, so there wasn't any rubbish lying around in the first place. Rachel hadn't said anything about wood piles, so that wasn't forbidden. When they were finished, the participants should all be able to fit in the den at the same time. There was no time limit, but this was a group of ambitious and purposeful individuals and they all agreed that they'd have the den finished in a few hours. It'd be child's play, they said.

Jim announced that he had always wanted to build a dry stone wall. Some of them were said to be several hundred years old, he told them, and it had always fascinated him as a child that these walls were nothing more than a few stones just lying on top of each other without any kind of binding agent: without cement, without mortar, or anything else like that. It really was unbelievable, he thought, that the only reason the walls were stable enough to stand fast through centuries of wind and rain was the stones' own weight. He was so excited to finally be able to try it out.

Liz seemed sceptical and said big stones would probably be too heavy to carry and lighter stones too small to build a proper wall, and besides they didn't have that much time or that much manpower – after all, they were all desk workers and weren't used to heavy labour. They'd do better to instead make sure they found enough wood; it wasn't particularly important, she said, whether the walls were stable and watertight and could hold for hundreds of years – it wasn't like they were going to live in it! Her idea was to ram a few bigger branches into the ground like pillars and then weave thinner branches and sticks between them. That'd surely be quicker than lugging stones around. Bernard was quick to agree with her and David shrugged his shoulders, nodding. Jim suggested he could start building a foundational wall using stones on one side while the others knitted the second wall from willow rods, and if he was too slow then they could always finish off the upper part of the wall with branches. But he really was very keen to give this thing with the stones a go, he added. That sounded like a good suggestion, David said. His efforts were all for peace and compromise, he'd had his fill of complications for the day.

Actually, what about tools, Jim asked, were they allowed to use them? If the boss was wanting to ram logs or even just a few thinner branches into the ground as pillars, it'd hardly be possible by hand – the ground was almost frozen, after all, and wasn't exactly soft. No idea, said the others, they'd have to ask Rachel, and did anyone know whether they were even allowed to ask Rachel questions as they went along? Oh please, Bernard weighed in, they were grownups, weren't they? And they weren't at school – of course they could ask Rachel questions and they could use tools, this was getting silly. Rachel, however, had disappeared. She had said she wanted to let the group get on with it for a bit and didn't want them to feel like they were under permanent observation. If that was the case, then they could make the decision not to ask her. Bernard was right, the boss decided, it was enough that they had to build the den in the first place. Privately she asked herself for the umpteenth time why she had even let herself agree to the ridiculous idea of a weekend away in the first place.

Unfortunately, right now they didn't have any tools though, David pointed out, asking whether anyone had any with them. And anyway, shouldn't they perhaps ask the McIntoshes first whether it was okay to build a den in their woods? Perhaps they wouldn't be keen on it at all. And if they were asking for permission, he added, then they could also take the opportunity to ask whether they could borrow some tools. Spades, picks, maybe an axe... Oh come on, said Jim, they didn't exactly want to chop down the forest! But if David was going, could he also ask about a wheelbarrow, please? That way Jim wouldn't have to lug each stone individually.

Of course, David hadn't meant it like that, he hadn't meant to volunteer himself yet again – but he accepted his lot as usual. Besides, the others thought of course that he was already acquainted with the McIntoshes' shovel.

By the time David returned – with wheelbarrow, spade, pick and official permission to build a den, granted by the delightful Aileen (the McIntoshes were both already at work) with an amused twitch of her lips – the others had already begun to gather the first sticks and stones. Jim was in as good a mood as ever, the boss as bad a mood as ever, and Bernard was bowing and scraping around her like a bark beetle around a pheromone trap. Sometimes even he noticed he came across as trying a bit too hard. But dear God, so he was trying! Which was more than could be said of some people. At the end of the day, he wanted a good career and that meant making an effort and getting the boss to notice you. Recently though, Bernard had realised it certainly wasn't only for professional reasons that his heart beat a little faster when Liz was nearby. Which merely added to his uncertainty.

Rachel and Mervyn remained out of sight. David asked himself how she was meant to observe the group's teamwork if she wasn't even nearby, but that didn't need to be his concern. No, his concern was the dead peacock and his deceiving the others, above all his boss; right now, he cared as little about this whole den thing as he did about the group's dynamics, roles and tasks. Really all he wanted was for this weekend to be over so that he could go home to his husband. But unfortunately, the weekend was just beginning.

Jim took the wheelbarrow and set off to find some stones. The dry stone wall was to run perpendicular to the wood pile.

The boss had assumed total control over the second wall – the one parallel to the wood pile – which surprised nobody, not even herself. For if she was honest, on the whole she considered all of her colleagues to be hopeless cases, with the exception of Andrew, who unfortunately was boycotting the den-building. Clever of him! Bernard, the little suck-up, would do whatever she said anyway, and David, well, hard to say – a nice enough guy and certainly not stupid, but insecure, and he somehow didn't seem particularly relaxed right now. Maybe he was simply too young to really be his own person yet. And Jim was just Jim – as constantly and enervatingly cheerful as if on drugs. How did he manage it, not letting anything ever upset him? How could an adult of sixty or so with so many brains in his head get that excited about stone walls? Surely that wasn't normal! Not to mention that old jacket and the unmentionable shoes he was wearing. Perhaps they were sensible, but what did he look like? They were here in a professional capacity, after all.

The boss carried a few smaller sticks and twigs to the place where they were building the den, letting Bernard haul the larger branches. She found his subservience dreadfully annoying, but if he wanted to play teacher's pet then go ahead, at least she could make use of it. She sent him away to fetch more sticks – thinner ones this time, please – to weave between the thicker branches. They had lodged the latter into the ground with the help of a spade. But this weaving lark turned out to be harder than expected. Liz got scratches on her hands, lost her patience and cursed the whole teambuilding weekend and the stupid shrink who she hadn't even really hired. She'd booked her old course-mate, because she'd figured if she really had to do something like this, then at least it could be with him; he had his feet firmly on the ground and couldn't be accused of anything too airy-fairy. There was nothing she despised so much as kumbaya. And then right at the last moment, he'd fallen ill, and she very much hoped for his sake that he really was ill and she wasn't going to discover someday that he'd cancelled because he didn't want to work with her crew. The colleague he'd sent in his stead was nice enough, but she clearly had some quite crude ideas. Building a den! They were bankers, not beavers! At least it had prompted the insight that she worked better with her head than she did with her hands and thus had made all the right decisions when it came to her career. Even if her squad was massively getting on her nerves right now. One thing she had to admit, though, was that it did smell better in the woods than it did in the bank. And certainly better than at that cottage they'd walked past with all that goose muck.

David cautiously pointed out that if they were just shoving sticks in the ground to make a wall, then surely it wouldn't be strong enough to bear the weight of a roof, and Liz had to admit he was right. Jim realised it probably would have been smarter to build the stone wall parallel to the wood pile, instead of perpendicular to it, but now it was too late. Somewhat irritated, Liz announced that they'd cross that bridge when they came to it and for now would just make the walls as stable as possible. David didn't think this a particularly sensible strategy, but he kept that to himself. In the end, they'd need to be able to lay a thick branch across strong corner pillars for the wall to bear the weight of a roof reaching all the way to the wood pile.

Bernard returned from collecting sticks and said that if the walls only consisted of sticks shoved into the ground, they'd hardly bear the weight of a roof. He didn't quite understand why his boss cut him off so abruptly and merely asked whether those branches were really all he'd gathered. Shortly afterwards, David muttered to him that they'd agreed to deal with the question of the roof later.

They were oblivious to the fact that Rachel had returned with Mervyn, still on his lead, and had been listening to them for a while. When they spotted her, Bernard asked how she was meant to assess the group dynamics when she wasn't even around. Rachel was genuinely surprised by the question and said it wasn't about her assessing anything and rather that the bankers were meant to find out for themselves how their group functioned. This was easiest when the context in which they were working changed, so when the same group worked together on a totally different activity. The aim was for them to gain a clear understanding of what was going on within their group set-up. She personally didn't have anything directly to do with it, Rachel explained, she was just facilitating the process. The boss rolled her eyes at all this theory and attempted to cope with yet another outbreak of sweat.

Nobody would have noticed Aileen going along the path downhill from them either – amused at the sight of the city folk's activities – if Britney and Albert hadn't stormed over to Mervyn, wagging their tails in delight. Neither the dogs nor Aileen understood why Mervyn had to remain on his lead. Aileen could see how well-behaved he was – besides, he'd been running around without a lead the day before. The fear that he might run away was clearly ungrounded, she felt sorry for the creature. The bankers conversely feared Albert and Britney might find the dead peacock wherever David and Helen had deposited it and were relieved when Aileen and the two dogs left. Aileen thought the bankers disagreeable, treating their dog so badly. She didn't like them, and she didn't see any reason to hang around exchanging pleasantries any longer.

Meanwhile, back at the house, Helen had managed to usher Andrew into the sitting room. First of all, she'd suggested he might like to take a walk, but he didn't want to come across the others building the den in the woods. In the end he'd have to take part after all and honestly, he said, it really wasn't to be countenanced. Helen was smart enough neither to agree with him in so many words nor to contradict him. So going for a walk was out of the question. After they'd made small talk for about an hour and drunk another coffee, she said she really needed to make a start on dinner for tonight and begin preparing the peacock for tomorrow. She said it intending to get rid of him, but instead he actually offered to help.

That really was very kind of him, she lied through her teeth, but the workspace here was a bit too small for two people; they'd constantly be getting in each other's way. He wasn't to take it personally, but she was most efficient when she worked alone. By the time she'd explained to him what she wanted done and how, she continued, she'd be quicker to do it herself. He was very welcome to just take a seat in the sitting room and do a bit of work on the computer or to lay and light the fire – she was sure the others would be glad to find the sitting room nice and cosy when they came back in from the cold woods later on. And so Andrew finally disappeared, although not into the sitting room at first but rather outside to use the wifi. While this meant she could get on with plucking the peacock, she was worrying the whole time that Andrew would come back into the kitchen and want something else from her, another cuppa or some sugar or something. To her relief, it wasn't long before she discovered he had indeed lit a fire in the sitting room and had then fallen asleep on the sofa. She had a bit of a weakness for sleeping men. And she had nothing against Andrew, but nobody else needed to know the peacock was a peacock and not a pheasant – and indeed that it was *the* peacock. It was bad enough that David knew. All of the others should continue in the belief that they'd buried the peacock in the woods and would be eating pheasant.

All the same, she remembered, someone else did know there had been a dead peacock in the woods – namely, whoever had shot it. Perhaps they'd simply been going to leave the bird to rot and wouldn't miss it. Otherwise they would have taken it with them, after all. But that wasn't overly plausible – why would anyone shoot a peacock if not to eat it? It could hardly be mistaken for pheasant or grouse. Whoever it was must surely have wanted to poach the peacock and then been disturbed, so that they'd had to leave the bird behind. Then again – who would do a thing like that? This Ryszard? His shop certainly gave the impression of a gourmet who appreciated something special, but she doubted he'd therefore relieve his employers of a bird unnecessarily. Although she didn't know him at all. But the Lady had spoken almost affectionately of him and had praised him and his shop to high heaven. No, that didn't fit with Helen's image of Ryszard. And the Laird and Lady weren't exactly likely to shoot their own peacock and then leave it lying in the woods. Aileen's broken arm disqualified her too. Somehow none of this made any sense – it must have been someone else, someone from the valley. And yet she didn't have the impression many people lived here.

Everyone in the construction gang had rosy cheeks by now, even Rachel, who kept coming back to check on the group and then disappearing again after observing them for ten minutes. Inexplicably, everyone was that bit nicer to each other during those ten minutes. Rachel took Mervyn, still on his lead, with her on her walks, and David in particular was pleased about this, as it meant the dog wouldn't discover the remains of the peacock after all.

Somebody certainly did make a discovery, however, and that somebody was Jim. Picking up some stones to put in the wheelbarrow for his wall, he uncovered a gun. For a moment he was startled, but then his brain clicked into gear. The gun didn't look like a modern weapon. The thing was almost historic, it might even be a museum piece, but at any rate it was really quite old and definitely wouldn't work any more. Jim came to the conclusion this must be some kind of facilitation game. It was a classic procedure after all – to first of all set an exercise and then build in disruptive factors – someone had told him that once. A group would, for example, be cooking something together and would have to go shopping, but an important ingredient would then be purloined from the supplies with the aim of observing how the group coped. Jim didn't just think this was idiotic but above all somehow unfair, yet he could imagine something like it being part of the den-building activity. Rachel had probably hidden the shotgun for one of them to find under the stones when she'd first gone for a wander and now wanted to observe how the group reacted to the find. He asked himself though how she'd brought the gun into the woods without them noticing. Beneath her jacket? Maybe. She was pretty well wrapped up. And why a gun in the first place? Where had she got it from? He looked around to see if Rachel was somewhere watching him, but he couldn't see anyone, neither Rachel nor any of the others. And being just as uninterested in mind games as everyone else and simply wanting to build his dry stone wall in peace, he put the gun back where it had been hidden and didn't say a word about it. He got on with building his wall and acted as if nothing had happened. Let Rachel go back into the woods again later and gather up her antiques! He briefly toyed with the idea of following her surreptitiously and jumping out on her, but he didn't want to risk the poor woman having a heart attack. She was only doing her job, after all, and she hadn't done anything to him. Besides, she was really nice. Jim was hungry, he'd take a look to see what was left of the provisions they'd brought with them. He'd probably already polished off most of them himself.

Rachel wasn't convinced the bankers were really getting as much out of building the den as she had hoped. One of them wasn't even taking part, which of course distorted the picture, and it seemed pretty obvious already who held which role within the team. Building a den didn't change that. Things weren't going so well overall – the bankers were proving remarkably stupid as far as constructing the walls was concerned and the general mood still wasn't great, although they weren't all bad sorts. But then it was for precisely this reason that she'd been booked. Unfortunately, the primary source of tension seemed to be the boss, which made the situation considerably trickier, for you could hardly tell her outright that she was the problem. This Bernard character didn't exactly help either, but she would have been able to deal with him.

Up until now she had mainly worked alongside her boss and she was still learning a lot from him. This group was a real challenge, but she resolved to approach it positively. She wanted everyone to be satisfied with her afterwards and to recommend her to other clients. But if she was quite honest with herself, she was a little nervous. She was also freezing; it was beginning to snow and it'd soon be getting dark. She and Mervyn returned to the site of the den, where the others too were wanting to return to the house.

They were just putting the spades and shovels in the wheelbarrow and about to set off when the Laird came through the woods with Britney and Albert and enquired as to how the den was coming along. The dogs had actually just been out with Aileen, but on arriving home, Hamish had heard about the den, and he didn't want to miss the sight of bankers doing manual labour. Besides, he wanted to make sure they hadn't discovered the dead peacock or the gun.

The investment department manager was visibly embarrassed at being caught building a den. Jim, on the other hand, proudly showed the Laird his stone wall, which might not look particularly impressive at first glance, he admitted, but he could already feel the work it had cost him in his bones. The Laird nodded, appropriately impressed, asked whether this was Jim's first dry stone dyke and complimented him. Jim said yes, until now he'd only read about building them and about the principle of double walls, which more or less leant against one another to achieve that remarkable stability. He had also read that a good craftsman could perhaps manage two yards a day but he wasn't a craftsman and hadn't ever done it before, so he'd decided just to build a simple wall after all and had found it hard enough to assemble suitable stones as it was. The Laird explained that in the double walls a tie-stone was added every few feet to connect the two walls and make for yet more stability, but before the two of them could lose themselves in shop talk, the ladies urged them to hurry up. It was snowing more heavily by this point. Now that they weren't working but were standing still and chatting, everyone was freezing and they were all looking forward to a nice hot cup of tea.

Hamish was relieved. When Aileen had told him the bankers were building a den he'd got a severe shock, but then he had thought the wood was probably big enough and they were unlikely to find either the bird or the gun. Had they found either of them, they'd surely have told him rather than philosophising about dry stone dykes. Besides, the den lay a wee distance away from the place where he'd hidden the dead peacock, if not quite as far as he might have wished. But he clearly didn't need to worry. The so-called den though! Ach well, city folk, the Laird said to himself, and office folk to boot! He kept the ridicule on the tip of his tongue to himself, and they walked back together. If he was honest, he was a desk person too after all and a bit clumsy when it came to anything hands on. And it was charming that this banker was interested in dry stone dykes, he thought. Even if he himself cared more for incunables.

The Laird stopped in a clearing. From here there was a bonnie view up through the glen to the north – you could see as far as the Highlands, where there had been snow on the ground for a few days already. The panorama was spectacular, the Laird could never get enough of this view. Could they see the small dark dots moving very slowly down from the mountains? he asked the group and passed around his binoculars. Those were deer – roes and red deer – hundreds of the creatures or more likely thousands. Their coming down from the Highlands in such hordes, he explained, meant there would be snow. A lot of snow, coming from the north, from the Highlands. Normally this happened in January at the earliest; he couldn't remember the deer ever coming down as early as November before, but at any rate the creatures were a reliable indicator that they could expect large quantities of snow. They please weren't to take this the wrong way, he said, by no means did he want to get rid of the group – but they should think about potentially setting off a bit sooner, perhaps even the next morning, for he simply couldn't guarantee that they'd even be able to make it out of the glen on Sunday. You never knew how long it would be until the snowplough came and cleared this far up the road. Ryszard would take care of the few miles of private drive down to the village, he said, but for the rest, they'd have to wait for the snowplough. His wife was already checking their supplies, they thought it very possible they might be snowed in for a few days.

The cook made tea for everyone. She quickly noticed a buzz of excitement amongst the bankers; apparently the Laird had predicted large amounts of snow. When Helen heard he even thought they might be snowed in, her first thought was that the peacock could then hang for a bit longer, that'd certainly do the meat good! However, she'd then also have to hide the bird for longer, which might prove difficult. But it would be wonderful for the meat, and that was the main thing. How much good it would do the bankers to spend more time together, she wasn't quite sure.

More than anything else, the boss would have liked to pack her suitcase and drive home there and then. This wasn't how she'd envisaged the teambuilding – if she was honest, she hadn't really envisaged anything, other than that she would have liked the coach to make a few things clear to her colleagues. She herself didn't really have anything to do with the team, after all: she was the boss. And now she was having to draw boats and build dens, while Mervyn killed other people's birds. No, this wasn't going well at all – she wanted to go home and felt unusually despondent. And because that simply wasn't an option and because she didn't like to admit defeat so quickly, she said it certainly wouldn't be that bad and she didn't see any reason to travel home sooner than planned. There was a very high-level meeting in the bank on Monday though which couldn't be postponed. If they really were snowed in, she was going to have a problem.

David too would have liked to set off early, as he had a guilty conscience and was scared of being found out, but he nodded along with the boss. It was his husband's birthday on Monday, David had booked the day off months ago. They were planning to go to Cambridge together, where they had first met. The two of them were going to have lunch and stroll around town before meeting up with old friends in the afternoon and going to the theatre in the evening. They had been looking forward to it for weeks.

Bernard's mind was suddenly filled with fantasies of sending the others home and letting himself be snowed in with the boss. There was nobody at home waiting for him or, as far as he was aware, for the boss. Out loud he agreed with her, it certainly wouldn't be that bad.

Andrew would have liked to travel home to his wife and children but held his tongue. He made an effort not to roll his eyes.

Jim was happy no matter what. He said he wasn't scared of a bit of snow, it was beautiful here, but he was also happy to go home. That clearly wasn't an option any more though. So Rachel and Helen didn't say anything either, although neither of them thought the Laird would have said something like that without meaning it.

Despite the somewhat tense atmosphere, everyone still meant well and so they assured each other this business about the snow was unnecessary scaremongering and it wouldn't get that bad. It was only November, after all, and their cars weren't so shoddy either, and it normally didn't get too bad on the roads anyway.

No one wanted to seem afraid of a little bit of snow. So they would simply continue the weekend as planned and travel home on Sunday. Andrew was the only person to eventually interject that the Laird had lived here for a while, after all, and presumably knew what he was talking about and might it not be smart to listen to him? This deer migration certainly sounded impressive, he said, and he for one had no desire to be stuck here any longer than necessary. Helen voiced her agreement, but the boss shot back that Andrew could forget it – there were good reasons why she had booked this weekend and now they were going to see it through, there was no point in him hoping to get home sooner. And anyway, she said, it wasn't all that cold, the little bit of snow would soon melt. She was rather surprised at her own vehemence. She was probably still annoyed by his refusal to take part in building the den and by the fact that he was presumably right about this too. He was smart, Andrew was, and he stuck to his guns. That impressed her.

That evening for dinner, as Helen explained to the bankers, there was a Chinese vegetable stir-fry with coconut milk, Thai-style vegetables with a peanut sauce, and a third, Japanese-inspired vegetable dish with miso, accompanied by a choice of buckwheat noodles or rice. She had even brought along chopsticks. The vegetables were crisp, the seasonings varied and all quite perfect, and everyone except Bernard tucked in with enthusiasm. Bernard made himself a stack of toast. His mood was on the floor – after the kind of work they'd just done in the woods, he wanted a proper steak and carbs, not this Asian vegetable mush. He was a banker, not a rabbit! Shaking his head, he opened another can of Irn-Bru. Helen ate on unmoved and remained at the table with the others. She didn't see it as her job to have her menus approved in advance or to fulfil additional requests. She had asked beforehand whether anyone was vegetarian or vegan or had any allergies, and her duty, she felt, ended there. Just because nobody was vegetarian didn't mean they had to eat meat every day. If the gentleman didn't fancy any of the three very different dishes, then please, let him eat toast.

Helen asked about the den, curious how their day had gone after all. Jim had evidently built a stone wall all by himself or had at least started to. He seemed content, as always, had clearly had fun and – as he said – had also learnt a few things about static equilibrium. The others had built a second wall from fallen branches, but before they could create a roof to cover the space between this wall and a wood stack, they had come home because it was beginning to snow and dusk had set in, and they were all freezing and hungry and didn't really know what to do about the roof anyway. The boss said that when it came down to it, she was a banker, not an architect, and incidentally, she had to admit that Andrew was absolutely right – this was kids' stuff and she was better at counting than crafting. She considered her share of the den-building at any rate to be done, even if the thing didn't have a roof. Rachel, however, said they'd wait to see what the weather was like the next day before deciding whether to continue building. Liz was impressed by the natural authority the young woman suddenly exuded. Rachel had noticed it too and was amazed herself.

Helen couldn't really imagine the boss had been a great help. She assumed she'd mainly been a backseat driver, telling everyone what to do and not contributing very much practically. She wasn't wrong.

Andrew couldn't believe the four had worked with vertical walls and had wanted to build a roof. Why on earth hadn't they planned slanting walls, he asked, that would have been much easier. They could have built something tent-like, and then they wouldn't have had the problem with the roof in the first place. They could have found a tree with broad, low branches, for example, and used the latter as beams, just leaning more branches up against them. Liz snarled that this was just super, not taking part in the first place and then knowing it all better afterwards. She was ashamed she hadn't thought of the idea herself, for of course he was right yet again. Jim took all the blame on himself, saying he had insisted on his stone wall, and a stone wall had to be vertical; no one had had a chance of suggesting slanting walls after that.

Bernard grumbled that he had calluses on his hands and he wasn't used to lugging heavy branches through the woods or digging holes to stick them in – he wasn't a builder, after all – and did any of the ladies maybe have some hand cream he could use? David just stayed quiet, he had withdrawn into himself. Helen couldn't have said whether this was due to the cold or the den or was still down to the business with the peacock. Or whether it was simply his nature.

Helen thought they all looked better for the rosy cheeks and fresh air, and if they hadn't all – with the exception of Jim – still been in very middling moods, the day could have been put down as a healthy change.

Rachel took this conversation as an opportunity to invite them all into the sitting room after dinner to briefly evaluate the den-building activity. During the evaluation it was stated that Jim had basically done his own thing and had done it well and with enthusiasm; admittedly alone and somewhat apart from the others, but nonetheless for the good of the whole. Further, that David and Bernard had mainly carried out the boss's instructions and that the boss had held back from any particularly strenuous physical activity. None of which surprised anyone. Andrew muttered quietly that that was a surprise and received a withering glance from the boss. Everyone made an effort to formulate these obvious statements as carefully and diplomatically as possible.

David secretly envied Jim his independence and the calm with which he let the boss's airs and graces bounce off him. He could see the boss respected Jim for this very reason, but he still didn't manage to act with similar confidence himself. He continued to give in easily and he knew this, and he also knew it wasn't good. And of course, he didn't say any of this but just silently wished he had some of Jim's integrity. The boss went straight into defensive mode and exclaimed that she certainly hadn't driven it home that she was the boss, but that she was the only woman there and the men were simply stronger. Plus, the men had more of a connection to nature, so it had been totally normal male and female behaviour; when it came down to it, David and Bernard were gentlemen. And anyway, she wasn't used to working in the woods, she might have injured herself – some of those things had had thorns, and on top of everything else, she'd been freezing. David and Rachel maintained an embarrassed silence, but Bernard piped up in agreement. You really couldn't expect a lady to do that kind of work, he had been happy to carry the heavier things for her. Liz was only just able to stop herself from rolling her eyes all too obviously. Jim, however, cleared his threat and said, well, actually, he certainly had felt she had made it very clear in the woods who was boss, as if the others would otherwise forget. It hadn't just been about physical labour, he said. Huffily, the boss insisted they were to please return to the meta-level; after all, the teambuilding was essentially about how they all behaved at the bank, and the fact was that she was the boss there, and it hadn't been the point of the den-building activity to change that in any way. And besides, she added, it takes two to order someone about – someone who's giving orders and someone who takes them. Bernard tried for appeasement, saying he hadn't felt ordered about, and Jim said nobody had said anything about anyone being ordered about. David thought his share, and Rachel finally understood – unfortunately learning the hard way – why she had always been taught that teambuilding could never take place in the presence of a manager, but only with team members who worked at the same level. She had known this, and her boss had most certainly known it. By now she really was beginning to doubt he was ill. He had known it, and he had known this particular boss, and he had landed Rachel with the job. And she had wanted to prove herself. How childish. She thought now. But she had to see it through – she'd manage and she would show her boss. And so before the situation could escalate, she said that, to conclude, everyone should please sum up in one sentence what he or she had learnt about themselves that day. Everybody rolled their eyes. Bernard spoke up and said he'd learnt that you couldn't just step out of the role you were used to at the drop of a hat, that it was damn cold in Scotland and that forestry work definitely wasn't his thing. The boss said she'd learnt that little games like this altogether weren't her thing and continued to sulk. Andrew had remained silent up until this point, as he hadn't even been there. He felt his decision had been validated and was glad he'd stayed at home. Finally, Jim said his realisation maybe wasn't particularly original, but for him the day had confirmed that even when you were in a team, you had to listen to your own heart and stay true to your passions – in the end, this was best not only for you but probably for the team as a whole too. David plucked up his courage and murmured that he'd learnt he maybe needed to find a stone wall himself, metaphorically speaking. These last two statements gave Rachel a glimmer of hope and gave Andrew and the boss at least something to mull over. Bernard didn't tend to mull over much anyway and when he did, it was only to wonder how he could make himself popular with the boss. After all, he wanted a good career, but he doubted this shrink and that ramshackle hut would in any way help him with that. But refusing to take part, like Andrew had, wasn't the answer either. And well, yes, not just because of his career.

One after the other, they all briefly disappeared. None of the men would have admitted it, but they were secretly turning on their electric blankets before returning with a drink from the kitchen. Beer for Jim, cider for Andrew, red wine for David, the boss stuck with tea. Bernard was still drinking Irn-Bru and had to put up with jokes about whether he was beginning to clog up inside. Andrew was the only person to ask the others whether he could get them anything too.

Jim put another thick log on the fire and fetched his guitar, which he'd brought with him to the boss's secret amusement. What was this supposed to be, she'd asked herself, some kind of campfire romanticism? *Take me home, country roads?* It was quite out of place, they were here to work after all. Teambuilding – all well and good, but singing together really was a step too far!

Just fifteen minutes later she'd changed her mind. Jim sang of whalers and shipwrecks, of unrequited and requited love, of murder and suicide, and particularly movingly of an old figurehead carver who felt a pride in and a passion for his work, which had been rather lacking for Liz lately. Sometimes she wished she could be just as passionate about her job, but then again, objectivity and a cool head were required in her line of work. *I will carve the music of the wind into the wood.* Sounded nice but it wasn't really called for in the bank. Though Jim had his passions too and they didn't get in the way of his work at the bank; quite the contrary, today he had made a remarkable contribution with his stone wall, and now it turned out he could sing too.

After Jim had put his guitar aside, they all headed up to bed one after the other. Bernard stepped outside for a bit. It was cold and still snowing. Bernard wasn't going anywhere, he just wanted to get some air. Sometimes he needed air.

Someone came out of the woods. Bernard automatically drew back into the shadows by the house, where he assumed he couldn't be seen. At first he could only make out a silhouette, but eventually he recognised the Laird. He was carrying a gun over his shoulder. These Scots had really weird customs – exactly what sort of animal did you hunt at night? The deer which had come down from the mountains? Surely not. Besides, the Laird wasn't carrying anything else, so he clearly hadn't shot anything. Then it occurred to Bernard that there must be foxes here which maybe went after the peacocks or the goose. Particularly when there was snow on the ground and the rabbits all stayed in their burrows and barely came out. Foxes were nocturnal, weren't they? Or did foxes hibernate? He didn't know and he didn't much care. He hoped it'd stop snowing so they could travel home on Sunday as planned. The Laird must have had a good reason to be coming out of the woods in the middle of the night with a gun over his shoulder. In the end, they were his woods.

After the Laird had disappeared into the house, Andrew came outside. What was he doing out here? wondered Bernard. He'd stopped smoking ages ago. Andrew said he just wanted to send his wife a quick message. Earlier, when the others had been building the den, he'd met the McIntoshes' housekeeper by the door, Andrew said, and she'd told him there really and truly wasn't any phone signal up here but he could use the open wifi. It didn't reach into the west wing though, so instead he had to go outside and stand near Lady Fiona's study.

Bernard didn't ask why Andrew wanted to contact his wife. He probably wanted to wish her a good night or something equally banal. Just a few weeks ago, Bernard had happened to be nearby when Andrew had been on the phone to his wife. He'd clearly been glad to hear her voice despite the fact that she hadn't exactly called at an opportune moment. He'd taken a couple of minutes to talk and laugh with her and was incredibly kind and relaxed. He'd almost been flirting with her, or so it had seemed to Bernard. And yet they'd been a couple for more than twenty years, their children were already teenagers. Bernard had rolled his eyes – stupid sweet talk, that really was ridiculous after such a long time! Not that he'd have found it less ridiculous if it hadn't been that long.

But the scene had preoccupied him. If Bernard was being honest with himself, Andrew hadn't been whispering sweet nothings; he wasn't at all the type for that sort of thing. He'd simply been pleasant and straightforward as he talked to his wife, seemingly unbothered by any kind of irritation and happy to hear from her, even though it hadn't been about anything special but was something quite ordinary, something they needed to organise to do with the children. At the bank, Andrew was noticeably less easy-going, and he wasn't generally an effusive guy otherwise. He seemed quite different with his wife, relaxed and carefree. In the end, Bernard had admitted to himself that it had been a long time since he'd spoken that pleasantly to his own girlfriend. Instead he tended to be annoyed and irritated in her presence. As she did in his. He felt she imposed upon him, she felt he ignored her. When one of them phoned the other, it was generally related to stress, to accusations, explicit or implicit, or at least there was a sense that yet another accusation might be in the air. Did he love her? Hard to say. Probably not. Not any more.

Shortly afterwards, Bernard had split up with his girlfriend and moved out. The news had got around the bank, but nobody knew Andrew's phone call with his wife was what had caused it. Why would they? No one had asked. And, of course, he wouldn't have told anyone anyway – it wasn't anyone else's business.

Bernard knew he probably ought to somehow be grateful to Andrew, but instead he held it against him. It was Andrew's fault Bernard had split up with his girlfriend, it was Andrew's fault Bernard was suddenly thinking about what he wanted from a relationship like a teenager, it was Andrew's fault Bernard was alone – and how come Andrew had such an amazing wife anyway, a wife who he clearly still thought was amazing after all these years and who thought the same of him? That was just weird!

Bernard went up to his room and barely spoke to David, who was lying in the lower bunk and reading. He climbed moodily into the upper bunk and had almost forgotten the business with the gun. He envied and resented Andrew, and he was glad not to have to share a room with him.

In the bed shared by the two women, there was rather more talking tonight than there had been the night before.

It didn't stop snowing all night. Liz opened her curtains the next morning only to get yet another fright. A huge, grey-brown something was squatting on the window ledge outside, right next to the glass. It got as much of a fright as she did, letting out a loud cry and jumping down from the window. It took Liz a moment to realise it had been a female peacock – a peahen? – and to figure out it was probably warmer by the window than it was outside, although it was unbelievably cold even in here, she thought. There were frost flowers on the windowpane, which was why she hadn't recognised the peahen right away. The frost flowers were beautiful, so delicate. She opened the curtains fully now, and the mounds of snow she could make out beyond the frost flowers drove her back into her warm bed.

Liz had never been able to stand birds. She found them revolting: birds stank and flapped and brought vermin with them, and on the whole, they were somehow unpredictable – and stupid. Stupidity was another thing she couldn't stand. Stupidity and birds. And what was wrong with the wretched things up here anyway? First there'd been the issue with the goose and its excrement when she'd arrived; and you couldn't set a foot out of doors without being attacked by the goose repeatedly; and then all these peacocks – first, one fell on her head, then Mervyn killed one, and now one was stuck to her window. This was all just weird, it was enough to make you paranoid. Damn creatures!

Then she pulled herself together. She was being silly, it wasn't the animals' fault. That was just what the goose was like, she'd experienced it a few times now – it'd waddle up, gobbling loudly and head outstretched, then Jim would normally give it a few stern but witty words and it'd head off, gobbling more quietly. No big deal – the stupid goose was nothing more than a stupid goose. It was different with Mervyn though. Liz couldn't quite believe he was stupid, but she simply couldn't understand what had got into him to make him kill a peacock. His hunting instincts must have run away with him. Nothing like that had ever happened before but, after all, they lived in a city – Mervyn had never met any peacocks. If she really thought about it, he hadn't ever seen a bird that big, maybe it was quite normal that he'd got in a bit of a state. And the peahen just now must have been freezing. You couldn't hold that against it – it was bloody cold, even in here.

The snow outside looked beautiful though. From her window she had a gorgeous view out into the valley. It was still snowing and it wasn't quite light yet, so all she could really see through the frost flowers was a snowstorm in front of a white expanse, but when it stopped snowing and the sun came out, this whiteness would be dazzling. Perhaps the McIntoshes would have a few pairs of cross-country skis they could borrow? That'd certainly be more fun than building a stupid den.

They probably wouldn't be finishing the den today anyway, given how it looked outside. But Liz definitely wanted to head out as soon as it stopped snowing and go for a lovely walk in the snow. She loved snow. She found it reassuring when everything was covered with this clean, white blanket, as if the whole world were made new.

Mervyn stood next to her bed wagging his tail. He wanted to go out too – he always wanted to go out, particularly right after waking up. Liz realised she must have come down with a cold; it was only now that she really noticed that she had a headache, a sore throat and a blocked nose. Hopefully just her dust allergies, she thought, but she knew she'd caught a chill the day they'd arrived – first getting all sweaty on that walk and then shivering in the shower. And the den-building yesterday hadn't exactly been beneficial either, for of course she'd worked up a sweat during that too, and then she'd been standing still and got cold again. But it wouldn't be too bad, Liz was tough. She assumed a brisk walk in the fresh air would blow the cold right out of her head. She resolved not to exert herself too much today so as not to get hot and sweaty again, not to get worked up and not to let herself be riled by Bernard. If she could have chosen, she'd have preferred to spend more time with Andrew.

In the room next door, Bernard woke up in his top bunk and needed to go to the toilet. He'd have preferred to get dressed first; the prospect of encountering his boss in the hallway while in his pyjamas appalled him. Although it'd be even worse to see her in her nightie! No, you shouldn't ever have to face your boss before you're dressed – but he needed the toilet and it was urgent. Unfortunately, he needed to get down from the bed first and that had been somewhat challenging the day before. Luckily, David was apparently still asleep. Bernard wanted to climb down the ladder facing forwards, but he couldn't hold on properly behind him. He missed a step, tried to catch hold of the bedframe, and fell with a scream and a loud crash onto the floor, which was surprisingly far away. Somewhat dazed, he lay motionless for a few moments. By the time he began to recover himself, David had of course woken up and was sitting – startled but upright – in the bottom bunk. The boss was standing in the doorway, also in her pyjamas, and he could hear the cook hurrying in their direction and Jim jumping out of bed next door. Mervyn came running up to him and tried to lick his face, and Bernard was only just able to defend himself. At the same time, the boss asked him if everything was alright, and as she did, Bernard realised it certainly wasn't. No, his knee really hurt. When he tried to stand up, his eyes filled with tears. How embarrassing! Lying on the floor in his pyjamas in front of the boss and blubbering because he'd fallen out of a bunk bed and couldn't get up. It didn't get much more mortifying than this. Bernard briefly wondered whether he'd have laughed if it had happened to somebody else, but as it was, he didn't find it funny at all – just painful and humiliating. My knee, he moaned. He somehow managed to pull himself up onto the edge of David's bed, where he certainly wouldn't have sat of his own accord. Particularly not with David still in the bed. Helen kneeled in front of him, pushed up his pyjama leg without asking, and regarded his knee. He was to try stretching out his leg and now bending it, she said, as confidently and resolutely as if she had spent her whole life examining battered male knees. Which maybe really didn't look much different to a piece of dead meat. Bernard stretched and bent his leg as best he could. It hurt like hell, but he could more or less do it – at least a bit. Nothing crunched or cracked, and Helen declared that he should rest and cool it; that was all they could do right now anyway, for if she understood rightly, the next doctor would be miles away, and outside there was an awful lot of snow. Bernard turned even paler and the boss withdrew to the bathroom. David offered to help Bernard get dressed. Bernard flinched. He certainly didn't want David to dress him, but he had to admit that he wouldn't manage it alone and it wasn't like he could ask the facilitator for help. Let alone the boss. But first of all, he desperately needed the loo.

When Liz and Mervyn returned from their morning walk, the house smelt of tea and coffee and even of freshly baked rolls – and Liz most definitely had a cold. On top of which, her mood had deteriorated somewhat. She had really enjoyed the sight of the snow, but it was quite deep, and she didn't have the right footwear with her. Of course, nothing had been cleared and the snow slid down into her walking boots. Snow in the countryside clearly wasn't the same thing as snow in London. And so she hadn't gone far at all but had just walked around the house with Mervyn and had noticed that her car was damaged. Evidently the side had been hit by a stone, but she couldn't remember hearing anything like that on the journey here. There were a few dents though and some scratched paint on the rear left wing, as if something had hit the side of the car. Liz simply couldn't understand when and how that could have happened, she would have noticed something like that. She hadn't moved the car since their arrival, so it must have happened before then. But why hadn't she noticed it when she was unpacking the car? Could anyone else make sense of it? she asked the group, and looked so sternly at each of the men in turn that they all had the feeling they'd somehow been caught out, as if they'd deliberately damaged their boss's car. Which of course they hadn't. Although one or two of them occasionally would have liked to. Everyone except Bernard and Helen went outside to regard the damage and stood by the boss's car at a loss. None of them could think how it might have happened.

Except for Rachel. Rachel remembered right away how one of the peacocks had launched itself at the blue tissue paper, and she wondered whether a peacock might attack a car too. A car was considerably bigger than a peacock. She kept her suspicion to herself though – it sounded far too outlandish, and she suspected the boss would just laugh at her. But she decided to keep an eye on the peacocks. After all, her own jacket was bright blue, and she wasn't sure whether or not she ought to be afraid of the birds. At any rate, she'd take care not to wander around outside on her own when she had the jacket on. Going back into the house, she stepped on the stuffed monkey, which she hadn't spotted beneath the snow. Disgusting thing!

Hamish and Fiona McIntosh watched from a safe distance through an upstairs window and didn't move a muscle, just in case. So – the bankers had noticed the damage the peacock had wreaked. Would they ask the McIntoshes whether they knew anything about it? Probably not – they hoped. It was still snowing, the cars' wheels were half buried in the snow already and the bankers hurried back inside. They pretty definitely wouldn't be able to drive home tomorrow as planned if it didn't melt quickly. And it looked as unlikely that it would melt anytime soon as it did that it would stop snowing.

Bernard sat side on to the table at breakfast with his leg resting on a chair and looked out into the driving snow, grumbling that they should have listened to the Laird and driven home after all – in the end, they really would be snowed in and would freeze to death in this medieval dump! Didn't he have an electric blanket in his bed? asked Helen, who received an angry glare in response and proceeded to make him up an ice pack. A fire was already crackling in the hearth and the smell of rolls was warming too. The boss saw no reason for complaint except for her own headache and the damage to her car, and she advised Bernard to give a cup of tea and a warm jumper a try – it wasn't as if they were in the bank. The other men made an effort to be affable and to pass the two invalids their breakfast things.

It was still snowing after breakfast. The flurries of snow seemed even thicker and the snowflakes even larger. There was no point in even thinking about finishing the den. The day progressed with flipcharts and pinboards, post-its in the shape of speech bubbles and brightly coloured sticky dots, blue-sky thinking, brainstorming, partner work and evaluation phases. The bankers created organisational charts and flowcharts on their laptops; they visualised working processes; they reflected, argued and compromised. They were even downright silly and descended into laughter during one of the brainstorming sessions, which Rachel found immensely reassuring.

This kind of work played to their strengths far more than the den-building had. Yes, it was exhausting and stressful and their heads were swimming, but over afternoon tea, they determined that they definitely were getting somewhere. They'd been working so intensely that they had asked Helen if they could delay lunch and have afternoon tea instead, which wasn't a problem as, in her words, she had only made a few quick sandwiches and salads anyway. The few sandwiches were remarkably cute little rolls, some homemade and others shop-bought, with different types of cheese and meat and fish and homemade hummus, and topped with fresh vegetables – tomatoes, cucumber, cress, basil and other herbs: a feast for eyes and palates. The men marvelled at the sandwiches. They'd expected a few pieces of sliced bread slapped together with egg mayonnaise, and that would have been enough for them – although not for the boss, who had frowned yet again when she'd heard there would just be sandwiches – but, of course, Helen made even a few sandwiches into a feast. She also kept bringing drinks, fruit and homemade baking into the sitting room, plenty of healthy and tasty treats. They were unbelievably well looked after; even Bernard had to admit that they really couldn't complain.

They all had the feeling they'd made progress, even if these weren't necessarily the kind of results they were used to at the bank. Their calculations didn't yet balance the books, so to speak, but then what they'd been working on weren't calculations – that was why they'd found the day so remarkably tiring. Equally tiring was Bernard. He'd found something to object to in everything and grumbled so constantly that at some point Jim had started to ironically anticipate his complaints, which eventually led to Bernard becoming fully recalcitrant and shutting up entirely. That suited everyone else just fine, as it made their progress easier. Liz was torn between her delight at the snow; her headache and rising temperature; her irritation about the damage to her car and Bernard's bad mood all because of a twisted knee; her remembered revulsion at the birds; and her astonishment at the intelligence, creativity and constructive work ethic of Andrew, Jim and David, which were entirely new to her. Perhaps the fever was making her soft. She was finding it hard to breathe too. And this headache!

David resolved to play chess with Bernard that evening, for Bernard was sure to win and that'd make him happy. David's attitude to Bernard had altered somewhat over the past two days, with pity replacing aversion. It must be awful to always be so bad tempered and tense, what a horrible notion! What kind of a life was that? At the same time, he asked himself whether this pity for Bernard was perhaps rather arrogant or patronising. Then he pushed that thought aside, for he really did feel sorry for Bernard. And it really was a shame about his knee. You could tell it hurt fiendishly just by looking at him – it had gone blue and was quite swollen, despite the ice packs which Helen tirelessly made for him. No wonder Bernard's mood was on the floor – and unfortunately, Jim's attempt to make him see the funny side had gone wrong, Bernard didn't have the sense of humour for that kind of thing. David took another biscuit and passed one to Bernard too.

It had continued snowing all day, but now it stopped and the last bit of evening sun came out from behind the clouds. Helen had been out with Mervyn before the afternoon tea and had let him off his lead, for, of course, she knew he hadn't killed the peacock and so wasn't likely to kill anything now either. He then really had chased a pheasant, but luckily the bird had been able to save itself by fluttering beyond a fence. Now, over afternoon tea, she encouraged the others to go out for a walk too. They could surely do with a break and it really was beautiful outside. Bernard wouldn't be able to join them, he was still sitting with his leg raised and an ice pack on his knee. Liz wanted to stay at home too with a hot honey and lemon and a warm blanket. She'd been feeling worse by the hour. She had used up a large portion of their supply of tissues over the course of the day and she had a headache and – by this point – almost certainly a fever, and she just wanted to lie down for a bit. Helen suggested taking a hot bath – she could make Liz a concoction of camomile, thyme and sage to add to the bathwater, it'd help against the flu she was coming down with. The boss thought this was nonsense – she'd have preferred something which actually worked, something from a chemist, but she didn't dare contradict Helen. No one could get to a chemist right now anyway and the prospect of a hot bath was actually quite appealing. She looked at the men and said, yes, a hot bath certainly would be lovely, and would the gentlemen mind her using their bathroom? Or would that upset their plans as to who bathed when? Three of the gentlemen immediately replied that of course the boss could use the bath. Only Bernard secretly thought it would serve her right if they were to deny her the bath now after she'd so high-handedly decided on the first day that the shower belonged to her. But he just muttered that he didn't mind either, even though, truth be told, his swollen knee meant he wasn't in the mood for generosity, particularly not towards the boss. At the same time, he almost felt a kind of glee that she wasn't feeling any better than he was, as if this created some bond between them which would never otherwise have existed.

And so, with a somewhat out-of-date newspaper under his arm, Bernard hobbled into the sitting room, which was still filled with display boards and flipcharts covered in the day's output, and the investment department manager ran herself a bath. Rachel, Andrew, David and Jim took Mervyn on his lead and went out into the snow. As they passed the trampoline, Rachel said it was a shame it was covered in snow, she'd have loved to jump around a bit after such a long day. David would have liked to as well but wouldn't have been brave enough. It would have been too embarrassing if someone had seen him. Although Jim didn't feel like jumping, he offered to clear the snow from the trampoline for them, but he lacked any kind of tool with which to do so. And nobody wanted to use their bare hands.

When they returned to the house from their walk, they met the Laird and Lady outside, who told them more snow was due to fall overnight, and that they shouldn't count on being able to drive home the next day. Did they have enough provisions or was there anything they needed? They had ample supplies themselves, they said, and if necessary Ryszard could bring more stuff from his shop with the Land Rover, they needn't worry. They were just to say if they needed anything. And, of course, they should come into the McIntoshes' kitchen and use the telephone to call home and the bank and let people know they'd be staying a day longer. At least a day. But it was meant to thaw again on Monday.

The four thanked them for the offer, which they'd certainly take them up on, and told the McIntoshes about Bernard's swollen knee and the boss's cold. They were given an elastic bandage, a decongestant ointment and some painkillers. If necessary, they could also try to take Bernard down to the doctor in the village in the Land Rover, said Hamish, but that really would be a bit adventurous today. The four-wheel-drive more or less managed up here, but going down to the village in this storm was hardly doable, even with the Land Rover – there was a pretty steep northerly slope which they'd rather not risk. The group thought Bernard's knee wasn't quite that bad anyway, he could still limp at least, it'd be okay. The cook had offered Bernard a cabbage compress, but he'd refused it, rolling his eyes. Which hadn't surprised her.

And also, the McIntoshes said, as compensation so to speak for being snowed in, they were heartily welcome to use the hot tub at the end of the great lawn behind the trees. The group hadn't even noticed the hot tub but were delighted by the offer. The Lady said they had plenty of dressing gowns they could lend folk. With all the snow, there was nowhere to put your things, she explained, and the hot tub didn't have a roof. They'd be best just to head over there in dressing gowns and walking shoes and to take plastic bags along for the dressing gowns. They just had to pull back the cover, she said, the water was warm.

Helen was pleased to hear they really wouldn't get away the next day. She had been counting on this and hadn't prepared the peacock, it was still hanging in the larder. It could now hang there at least a day longer, that'd do it good.

Liz was still in the bath. It was beautifully warm; she simply lay there and did nothing. She had read for a bit, but then she put the book aside and just looked out of the window as it gradually grew darker outside. The only sound she could hear was the boiler heating up water for the next person who wanted a bath. She refilled the tub twice with hot water. The bath was doing her good. It was pitch black outside by the time she heard the others return but she didn't want to get out yet – she just wanted to lie in the warm water a little longer, even though her fingers were already wrinkly. At least the hot, herby steam meant she was able to breathe a bit better.

Helen knocked cautiously at the door. Yes, called Liz, everything was fine, she just wanted to stay in the water a little longer. Andrew had very politely inquired as to whether he might possibly use the shower in the other bathroom, Helen called through the closed door, and the boss called back, goodness, of course he could! Somehow, she no longer quite understood why she had divided up the bathrooms so categorically on their arrival, it was a bit silly given that they were all grownups. A teambuilding weekend wasn't a school trip!

Rachel and the men had been outside for a while and were now all thoroughly frozen through. They turned on the fan heaters in all the rooms. Helen put the kettle back on with enough water to make everyone a cuppa, and a soup was simmering on the stove. Andrew showered, making use of the new unit's instant hot water, the boiler in the other bathroom was heating up the next tubful, and Jim was feeling peckish again. He went into the kitchen. Helen gave him two slices of bread, and as he pushed down the knob of the toaster, there was a loud bang and then everything went dark.

Jim started. That must have been him, he said, and asked Helen, who was standing next to him, whether she knew where the fuse box was.

Helen started and replied that there were some thingamabobs up high in the larder, just beneath the ceiling, but they looked pretty prehistoric to her. They couldn't have been operational any time recently, there must be a newer fuse box around somewhere.

Liz started and stayed where she was. A fuse must have blown, the others would find the fuse box and flip it back. She certainly wasn't going to try to climb out of the bath, get dry, fumble for her things and so on in the pitch black.

Andrew started twice: once when there was a sudden bang and everything went dark, and then again when the shower water all at once turned icy cold. He swore and climbed cautiously out of the shower. Dripping wet and naked, he felt around for his towel which was lying on the floor, and when he stood up again, he banged the back of his head against the cupboard door above the sink, which had opened silently. He yelped, dried himself, got dressed shivering, and realised he had a bump swelling up on the back of his head.

Lying on the sofa in the sitting room, Bernard started. He was a little scared of the dark, but the fire was still crackling away, so it wasn't too dark at all. His knee hurt. He pulled the blanket up around him and stayed where he was. The others could deal with this, thank you very much! He was going to stay here and look at the fire.

David was in his room. He started, waited briefly to see if anyone else would say anything, and then called out that he was sure he'd find his phone in a moment; that'd at least give them a bit of light until they could find the torch the Laird had given them in case they wanted to go outside at night. Helen called back that there were also candles in one of the kitchen drawers, and did Bernard have the matches in the sitting room?

David found his phone and used it to light his way to the front door. The torch was meant to be around here somewhere. The snow outside reflected the last of the evening light, and their eyes gradually got used to the dark, so that they were soon all able to make out a bit more.

Helen searched for the candles, and Jim felt his way into the sitting room where Bernard, still lying on the sofa, told him the matches were on the very left of the mantlepiece. They heard Andrew swearing loudly from the bathroom.

Rachel came out of her room, lighting her way with her mobile as well. She met Jim in the sitting room and lit the way to the kitchen for him. They lit a few candles in the kitchen, and just as Jim was wanting to go into the larder with a candle to look at the fuse box, David came back with the torch.

Helen wanted to prevent Jim from looking at the fuse box, as the peacock was also hanging in the larder, the peacock which was noticeably larger than a pheasant – there was nothing she could do about that. Jim wasn't stupid, he'd wonder what kind of large bird was hanging there and he'd put two and two together. Helen had always answered the odd question about the meal plan by saying they should wait and see, and she was no longer sure whether she'd mentioned to Andrew that there'd be pheasant. And perhaps he'd already told the others. Luckily, David wasn't stupid either – he figured out quickly enough that nobody other than he and Helen was allowed to see the peacock, and he went into the larder to look at the fuse box himself. The box was pretty high up and David couldn't really discern much in the torchlight. What he did see, though, looked to him to be so old that they couldn't possibly be the current fuses, he was sure there had to be newer ones somewhere. In the end, Jim did take a look at the fuses too, but apparently didn't notice the peacock. Luckily, it was hanging on the wall opposite the fuse box, almost behind the door.

Jim and David traipsed through the west wing with a candle and the torch but couldn't find a more modern looking fuse box and decided to ask the Laird. Maybe there was a central fuse box somewhere. It only occurred to them now that the power might have gone off at the McIntoshes as well, but it turned out that wasn't the case, as there was light in their windows. Meanwhile, in the kitchen, Helen and Rachel dripped wax onto saucers to stand candles on them, and then placed them around the room. Rachel took a candle into the sitting room for Bernard, even though the fire gave off enough light – she felt he could do with a friendly gesture. She didn't have any light herself on the way back and had to feel her way along the hallway, almost sweeping a picture off the wall. Then she left candles in front of the bathroom doors for Andrew and the boss and called through the doors that they shouldn't stumble over the candles when they came out. Andrew was half-dressed by now and mumbled a thanks through the door, while Liz announced that she'd simply stay in the bath until the light was back on.

First of all though, she decided to refill the bath with hot water, only to discover that there wasn't any left. She had used up the entire contents of the boiler and now no new water could be heated up. If she wanted to stay where she was, then the power had better come on again soon, but that wasn't likely to be a problem. Flicking back a fuse switch wasn't exactly rocket science.

Except that it was. Jim and David knocked at the McIntoshes' back door, which led into the kitchen. The Lady opened the door and invited them in, as it was snowing again outside, and the snow was drifting in. She closed the door behind them, and they quickly assured her that they didn't intend to stay but had simply wanted to ask for the Laird, as a fuse had blown in the west wing – they hadn't found the fuse box and were wondering where it was. Lady Fiona snorted a bit to herself at these unemancipated city folk. The Laird, she explained, was a classicist, nobody would want him to go anywhere near the fuses! That she was an engineer she kept to herself. Hamish might be able to shoot a peacock, but his technical expertise ended there. She kept that to herself too. The fuses, she said, were in the larder and, well, they weren't quite as old as the whole house but they certainly had a good vintage, which meant that the fuse hadn't blown but had burnt through. This wasn't particularly good news, she explained, as the historic fuses were rather hard to come by, and they'd recently used up the last spares they'd had. She'd have to try to bridge the whole thing with a piece of electric fencing wire, but she couldn't make any promises. They'd need, she said, a good torch, a piece of wire, some tools and the gas soldering iron – Aileen would help her to gather everything together. Luckily, the main part of the house had its own power circuit, which wasn't connected to that of the west wing, so all of the lights there were still on. And they ran on 230 volts. The west wing still ran on 110 volts, she explained. It was high time to replace the whole thing but, well, it came down to cost. Most electricians didn't even know where to start with the old fuses and 110 volts, she said. What she didn't say was that she'd need to climb a ladder to get to the fuse box. Bridging a burnt fuse with a piece of fencing wire wasn't a problem for her. But she was a wee bit scared of heights.

Lady Fiona briefly considered whether she should move the whole group elsewhere but decided against it. None of the cottages were big enough to fit all of them, she'd have had to distribute them between several cottages a few miles apart from each other. Plus, Aileen wasn't able to pitch in and the cottages weren't all ready for guests. To say nothing of the fact that the heating hadn't been on, and there was so much snow on the ground that they wouldn't get there with the cars. She would have had to ask Ryszard for help, and it would be considerably more faff than simply bridging the burnt fuse. The bankers apologised for the bother for the umpteenth time. They really were sorry, they said, they'd probably just been using too many devices at once: several fan heaters, the shower unit, the boiler, the stove, the kettle, the toaster – it must have been too much for the electrical system, they hadn't even given it a thought. But could they make themselves useful in any way? Aileen was helping to gather a few things together, she knew where everything was but couldn't do much with her arm in plaster and had to limit herself to giving directions. The bankers helped her as best they could.

This was exactly what Helen, back in the west wing, was afraid of: what if the ancient fuses were still in use after all, meaning someone would soon look in the larder and see the plucked peacock? She took off her apron and – by the dim candlelight which reached the larder from the kitchen – hung it next to the dead bird, so that the peacock was half hidden behind it. She hoped no one would pay it any attention. So far, everyone had enjoyed the food and eaten enthusiastically, but nobody had been particularly curious about the contents of the larder. Everyone ate what she put on the table. Everyone except Bernard, of course.

It was pretty dark in the bathroom, and the investment department manager lay in the bath and realised the water was slowly getting colder. Then it occurred to her that the fan heaters and the heated towel rail wouldn't be working any more either, and so the air in the bathroom would also be cold by now, and that she should get out of the bath, get dry and put some warm clothes on as quickly as possible. And then for a nice hot cup of tea.

A sliver of moonlight was shining on the snow outside, making for a soft shimmer of light in the bathroom too. It wasn't snowing as heavily any more. Shivering, Liz got out of the bath and reached for her towel. She towelled herself down, felt around for her clothes and swiftly got dressed in the dark. She was freezing again, her nose had immediately blocked back up, and she still had a headache and a sore throat. She was going to get into bed with a cup of tea, she decided, and then it occurred to her that no electricity meant no tea, and the electric blanket wouldn't be working either. Nor would her hairdryer. Going to bed with wet hair when she had such a bad cold didn't sound like a good idea. Perhaps she'd be better to twist a towel around her head and sit by the fire, wrapped in her duvet. With the men who were her employees. Next to Bernard and his swollen knee. What sort of an impression would that make?

Meanwhile, Andrew had got dressed in the other bathroom and had knocked over the candle in front of the door after all, dripping some wax onto the floor. He went to join the others in the kitchen. He too was shivering, and he too only realised at the last moment that there wouldn't be any hot tea.

Just as Jim and David were about to set off back to the west wing together with the Lady, Ryszard arrived in his four-wheel-drive, which was more or less equal to the snow. He'd brought Lady Fiona half a dozen eggs and some vegetables – she'd phoned him to ask for them. He also wanted to check the McIntoshes were alright. Everyone looked out for each other in a community this small. He told them he'd cleared the snow from the roof of his shed so it wouldn't collapse. Hearing this, Lady Fiona wanted to know if he'd been well secured so as not to risk falling off the roof or collapsing through it together with the snow. Ryszard side-stepped the truth somewhat in his answer so that Lady Fiona wouldn't worry, and as he'd expected, she then asked him to maybe clear the snow from their garage roof too when he had a moment. Otherwise she could do it herself, of course. Sure, he'd be happy to, said Ryszard, but maybe he should take a look at the burnt fuse in the west wing first? He needed to drop by so they could pay for yesterday's purchases anyway. Ryszard was a nice guy – he knew perfectly well that Lady Fiona was more than capable of soldering a piece of fencing wire to the fuse. He also knew she didn't like climbing ladders. All of a sudden, Aileen wanted to go to the west wing too – she liked being in Ryszard's company. Out loud she said that maybe she could make herself useful after all, checking on the invalids or something. Besides, she thought, she wanted to make sure the bankers weren't mistreating that dog again.

And so Ryszard, Lady Fiona, Aileen, David and Jim set off back to the west wing, with a small toolbox and all sorts of torches and paraffin lamps. Helen, Rachel and Andrew were waiting by candlelight in the kitchen, Bernard was still lying on the sitting room sofa, looking into the fire, and the boss had just come out of the bathroom, a towel wrapped around her wet hair, and asked if there were any tissues left. She sounded really ill now and looked it too, as far as they could tell in the dark.

Ryszard stepped into the larder. Helen turned away, wishing she were no bigger than a mouse. She didn't want to see what would happen if he or the Lady discovered the dead peacock. But it was still dark in there. Ryszard put up the ladder in the doorway, asked Jim to shine the torch on the fuse box, unscrewed the burnt fuse and sat down with it at the table. Which was a bit of a relief – but he'd have to go back into the larder to screw it in again.

Aileen barely had to look to hand Ryszard the tools he needed, she knew where everything was in the toolbox. Meanwhile, Lady Fiona satisfied Jim's curiosity by explaining how everything functioned: the old electricity network on 110 volts, and the new one on 230 volts, how it all hung together and how they corresponded with one another – or rather didn't.

The men were impressed by the Lady's expertise, while Liz marvelled above all at Jim's thirst for knowledge. But this flu really was taking it out of her. She asked Helen whether there were any lemons left and whether, once the power was back on, Helen could bring her a mug of honey and lemon in bed. There were a couple of lemons left but she was running low, answered Helen, but she'd be happy to press her some orange juice too, vitamins were always good. Lady Fiona promised to look in her medicine cabinet when she got back, she was certain she'd find something for flu. And she had several lemons which they were welcome to as well. And did they have enough tissues? She took the opportunity to ask after the other invalid and his knee, and Aileen tapped at her plaster cast, exclaiming that they might as well be a field hospital – but no one else was in the mood to laugh. Andrew said, speaking of which, was there any ice left? – he had hit his head so hard on the bathroom cabinet that he was getting a bump. Aileen was just about able to keep from laughing, and Helen asked him to wait a moment until the lights were back on and then she'd make him an ice pack. And she'd make another for Bernard's knee while she was at it. They were all freezing – everyone really would have preferred to be thinking about hot soup, not about ice packs. The soup on the stove was going cold.

Liz apologised rather formally, wished everyone a pleasant evening and retired to bed. She would probably be better off there, she said stuffily. Her nose was quite raw by now, and she was sure she'd get a cold sore next, that always happened. It was so stupid her getting ill here – she had wanted to work with the men, not lie uselessly in bed, being waited on hand and foot. She never got ill normally, and this really was an inconvenient time to start; she was the boss after all, what sort of an impression did it give if she just disappeared off to bed? But she didn't have a choice – joining Bernard on the sofa wasn't an option either. She was pretty sure she had a fever now, and her knees were quite weak. And she was cold. She took a candle with her to her room, put it in the window, laid the bedspread over both of the duvets and got into bed.

Mervyn was confused. He ran back and forth and realised something wasn't right but couldn't understand why nobody would turn the lights on, and why his mistress was going to bed before he'd had his dinner. He stood by her bed, looking at her expectantly, and tried wagging his tail a little, but she just murmured that he should lie down. Mervyn obeyed, but he didn't understand why he wasn't getting anything to eat before going to sleep and why he was meant to go to sleep now at all. Not that he had anything against sleeping at any time of day, but just now something wasn't right. Perhaps he could ask the woman in the kitchen for something to eat later, she seemed to be a highly capable human. She was the only one here who let him off his lead. And she smelt good too.

Ryszard soldered a piece of wire to the fuse, causing a considerable stink. David asked what would happen now – would the fuse work or was there anything they needed to watch out for? Jim illuminated the fuse box with the torch again, the peacock – drawn and ready for the pot – hung diagonally behind him, half hidden by the cook's apron, and Ryszard explained they should be even more careful now, because the wire he had soldered to the fuse was much thicker than the real fuse wire. That meant, he continued, that it wouldn't burn through; in the worst-case scenario, if the wires were overwhelmed, they would begin to glow and then catch fire. Which was what a fuse would normally prevent. He was screwing the fuse with its makeshift repair back into the box as he said this, and all at once, the lights, kitchen radio, fan heaters, boiler, instant water heater and electric blankets all came back on. The group agreed to turn off a few heaters and concentrate for now on heating the kitchen and sitting room, where the fire really gave off enough warmth anyway, and to pay attention going forward to how many electrical devices were on before turning on another. Absolutely nobody wanted to risk an electrical fire. They were thus all preoccupied by the electricity, and nobody paid any attention to the dead peacock in the larder. Andrew and Jim only had eyes for the old fuses and perhaps hadn't even noticed the bird. Helen breathed a sigh of relief and asked Ryszard what she owed him for the vegetables she'd fetched from his shop. She started a conversation about planting vegetables, what he cultivated and when, and what he bought and how he planned it all, during which she discreetly closed the larder door and got to work making an ice pack for Andrew. They had just about got away with it.

Dinner was soup, which warmed them all up again, followed by a delicious homemade steak pie with lots of fresh vegetables and potatoes and gravy made from red wine, rosemary and thyme. And for pudding there was a trifle so good it prompted a spontaneous proposal of marriage from Jim. The boss was in bed. She was grateful for the bowl of soup which Helen brought her and ate it all up. Utterly exhausted, she then fell asleep right away. When Helen returned with the main course, she was already snoring in a rather unladylike fashion. Helen let her sleep. The men seemed a little more relaxed without their boss around, she thought, but perhaps that was down to the snow or to making it through the shared adventure of the power cut.

After dinner, David said he'd quite like to take up the Lady's offer of the hot tub. Did anyone want to join him? Rachel impulsively said yes, but then realised none of them were likely to have brought swimming togs with them, meaning they'd have to be naked. Well, if it wouldn't bother him, she added, then, well… and David hurriedly assured her it wouldn't bother him at all. To everyone's surprise, Andrew said he'd join the two of them. Jim and Helen wanted to stay where they were and Bernard, who they asked out of politeness, just rolled his eyes. He lay back down on the sofa, ice pack on his knee, and stared into the fire. Jim brought him a pot of tea. Lady Fiona had also brought over a few books and newspapers and so it was quite cosy really, he thought, and his knee was feeling a bit better too. At least he was mobile enough to occasionally put another log on the fire.

David, Andrew and Rachel borrowed dressing gowns and towels from the McIntoshes and tramped across the snowy lawn, wearing just the dressing gowns and their walking boots. They took Mervyn with them on his obligatory lead. Rachel thought the general mood really was astonishingly relaxed, not just in comparison with the atmosphere on their arrival but also given that they had to stay a day longer than planned, that Bernard's knee was clearly really painful, that the boss didn't just have a bit of a cold but a serious flu, and that they weren't surrounded by the luxury they were used to – instead, everything was noticeably simpler and more makeshift than in the bankers' own homes. Now and then there were small moments of irritation, but on the whole they were all amicable, sometimes even downright cheerful. And, above all, they were noticeably less tense than they had been two days ago. Which must in part be thanks to Jim and Helen, whose imperturbable good moods slowly but surely seemed to be infecting the others.

On the way to the hot tub, David remembered with a guilty start that he'd wanted to play chess with Bernard. Now Bernard was lying alone on the sofa yet again – but maybe Jim would keep him company. If he didn't choose to remain with Helen, who was certainly a more pleasant companion. Bernard's mood had been somewhat better since he'd split up with his girlfriend, but now, with his knee in pain, it had turned black and he was almost unbearable. Crossing the large, snow-covered lawn, their feet sank so deep into the snow that it slipped down inside the tops of their walking boots. It was cold and wet and ticklish, and David began to giggle. Rachel joined in and even Andrew was amused. They started walking faster so as not to be entirely frozen through by the time they arrived at the hot tub, with the result that even more snow slid into their boots, making them giggle even more. They were cold but they were having fun. They agreed that Mervyn surely wasn't about to kill another peacock or anything else for that matter and let him off his lead. If he had to sit still by the hot tub all the time they were in it, he'd get cold himself – it'd certainly be better if he could move around a bit. The decision made them feel rather audacious.

By the time they'd figured out how to work the locks on the hot tub cover in the dark and had folded it back, they were so cold it was no longer quite as fun. Suddenly, Andrew was uncomfortable with the idea of getting undressed in front of Rachel and David after all. The sky was clear, the moon and the snow offered a little bit of light, and they could see remarkably well. It didn't bother David at all, however; he was an athlete and used to getting undressed in front of other people. He took off his dressing gown, stuffed it into the plastic bag which held his towel, hung the bag from a branch and climbed down into the warm water. Rachel imitated him but made an effort to turn away a bit, and so eventually Andrew decided it didn't matter and joined the others in the hot tub. They each found a seat in one of the corners, and for a while, they didn't say anything at all. They simply lay in the warm water, looking up into the starlit sky, listening to the rustling of the undergrowth, letting the warmth of the water permeate their bodies and attempting to ignore the biting smell of chlorine. Beautiful, one of them sighed, and the other two murmured in agreement. Now and then, one of them would call Mervyn, who always came trotting back immediately; he never went very far and didn't give the impression of being on the hunt for peacocks. David briefly climbed out of the hot tub and fetched a hip flask from his dressing gown pocket. It had Drambuie in it, he said, did anyone want a sip? Rachel had never been exactly sure what Drambuie was. It was something Scottish, David said, a whisky liqueur with honey and herbs or something. It made you smile at any rate, she should just try it. Rachel took a sip; it was sweet but powerful at the same time. Andrew and David looked at her expectantly, and she smiled. There you are, said David, and Rachel passed Andrew the hip flask, beaming. Andrew marvelled at David, usually so shy and reserved, who all of a sudden was almost casual and confident, undressing in front of him and a woman they barely knew and passing around alcohol. Andrew had always liked David, perhaps precisely because of his shyness. He was perfectly aware he didn't come across as particularly easy-going himself. He sometimes wished he could be a bit more laidback, but then he'd tell himself that he just wasn't and that was okay. But given that he was currently naked in a pool with a colleague and a woman he didn't know, and to top it off, had a big bump on the back of his head, he felt amazingly relaxed. He leant back, passed the hip flask on and looked up into the sky. Mervyn was snuffling about behind them. They asked themselves whether he could even smell anything in the snow and whether his feet might be getting cold, but he clearly didn't mind.

The Drambuie hit Rachel first. She wondered aloud what all the buttons at the front of the hot tub were actually for and pressed one. A light went on beneath the water and all three of them suddenly felt considerably more naked than they had before. Rachel quickly turned the light off again and pressed another button, which turned on the whirlpool. There was suddenly a loud bubbling – air came out of unexpected holes in the walls and floor, and all three of them were briefly lifted from their seats by the churned-up water and pushed in directions they hadn't anticipated. The hot tub was suddenly very small; skin encountered skin, limbs drifted any which way, hands and arms brushed against other bodies, feet and legs brushed against other feet and legs, and none of the three quite knew who they had just touched and where and who had just touched them, and none of them could have said if the hot tub was too small or just small enough. None of the three found these moments of touch unpleasant, but none of them would have admitted that. Truth be told, they would all have liked it to go on for a bit longer if that hadn't been impossible. They all yearned for physical contact, but all three of them assumed they were alone in this desire, and so they pretended to go back to their places and to get away from each other as quickly as possible.

Rachel's last boyfriend had split up with her a few months ago and that was for the best. On the whole she was content being single for now, she didn't necessarily need a man to be happy. With the set-up here though – being on her own without any colleagues, and with her role as facilitator meaning she didn't directly belong to the group – she was suddenly overcome with loneliness and a yearning for human touch. She would have liked to just nestle up to one of the men, or to both of them, she found them both quite attractive in their own ways. But of course, that wasn't an option, she had a role to play here. Although the roles seemed to be blurring in the dark and the snow. Nonetheless.

Andrew was happy in his relationship with his wife. He'd spent half his life with her, he loved her, but some things weren't quite as exciting after half a lifetime. Brushing against the limbs of strangers, however, was exciting, the young psychologist was very pretty, and David was a man, a naked gay man. Andrew had never touched a naked man before and he would never have believed that doing so wouldn't bother him, that he might even find it pleasant. Something tickled his lower leg, someone's thigh or just a jet of air, how could you be sure? His heart beat a little faster. Luckily it was dark.

David was very happy with his husband too. They'd only been married for just over a year and he was the happiest he'd ever been, but that had absolutely nothing to do with the fact that at this moment he yearned for human warmth and human skin. Everything was different beneath the water and in the dark.

What happened in the whirlpool had nothing to do with their everyday lives. There was only them and the warm water and the stars and the skin of the others.

Rachel turned the whirlpool off. The men laughed self-consciously, and she said it had been a bit too loud, hadn't it? – and it was so nice and quiet out here. And the men agreed with her. Then they grew quiet again and sensed the ghosts of each other's touches still tingling, and more than anything else they would have liked to turn the bubbles back on to let themselves be touched again. They all sighed silently and asked themselves whether their legs were still tingling from the bubbles or whether that was someone else's leg after all and – if so – whose, but they didn't dare move to find out.

Andrew was the first to speak. He knew an astonishing amount about the stars, and you could never see them this well in London. He pointed up somewhere into the dark – and so that they could better follow the line of his arm, David and Rachel slid nearer to him, and because water carries, they ended up touching again, and they acted as if nothing was happening or as if they hadn't noticed, and then they slid a bit further away after all, and Andrew tried to explain things using words instead. David only knew the Great Bear, Rachel knew Cassiopeia too but that was it. The Milky Way was clearly visible. Andrew showed them Andromeda, Aldebaran, Orion and the Pleiades. He talked about Castor and Pollux, Lyra and Pegasus – and he knew how many light years away they all were, and which stars had long since been extinguished but would still be seen for hundreds of years because the light was still travelling. He showed them Uranus, which was always easier to see in the first half of the night. And then they all went quiet again, because sometimes you just go quiet, and they passed the Drambuie round once more and looked up into the sky, and nobody really knew what was actually happening beneath the surface of the water. It was warm and quiet and peaceful, and at some point, their fingers went wrinkly and they climbed out of the water and dried themselves quickly – and it was still warm, and they put their dressing gowns on, and it was still a little warm, and they called Mervyn who didn't come back. They put on their walking boots, which were wet inside because of the snow sliding into them, and immediately got icy cold feet, and then they closed the cover of the hot tub and no longer felt quite as warm. They ran through the deep snow across the lawn clumsily, their laces untied, and it was warm and cold at the same time. And more than anything, they would have liked to cheer and fall down in the snow, and even more than that, they'd have liked to jump around on the trampoline – but they were adults and it was cold and there was snow on the trampoline. And they didn't have any clothes on. They called Mervyn, but quietly, because they weren't really meant to have let him off the lead, and they didn't want anyone in the house to hear them calling. Mervyn arrived from an unexpected direction, and they jokingly asked him whether he'd gone and killed something after all, and they put him back on the lead for the last few metres to the house.

Back in the west wing, Jim took a fresh ice pack and a cup of tea into the sitting room for Bernard and asked whether he'd like some company. Bernard thanked him but said that wasn't necessary, he was quite content alone on the sofa with a few newspapers, so Jim was welcome to join the others going to the hot tub – which Jim had absolutely no desire to do. Somewhat relieved, Jim went back into the kitchen and helped Helen finish clearing the table and drying the dishes. Helen half-heartedly tried to tell him this wasn't necessary, but she was glad to have such good company. They were soon deep in an animated conversation, which took them from dry stone walls, via the creatures in the woods, to cooking and food, and then onto the house's two invalids. When they were finished with the dishes, Helen asked if they should go into the sitting room and keep Bernard company, but Jim told her Bernard had said thanks but no thanks, and instead he fetched his guitar. Helen checked on the boss, who was half awake, and while she was there, she asked whether it would bother Liz if Jim were to play guitar for a bit. Oh no, said the boss, quite the contrary. Jim sang so nicely, she liked hearing him sing, and she was sure it wouldn't stop her from falling back to sleep. Helen raised an eyebrow in spite of herself. Liz was just to say if it got too loud, she said, and returned to the kitchen. It turned out Helen was a good singer herself and knew many of the old folk songs too, and those she didn't know, she quickly picked up when Jim showed her his folder of typed-up lyrics. They thumbed through it together, picked out one gorgeous song after another, and spiritedly discussed what singers had recorded which songs. They sang in harmony and soon stopped worrying about whether they were too loud, because some lines and choruses were just meant to be sung loudly – because sometimes things just have to break out of you, and because we normally don't allow ourselves to be loud. And then they sang quietly again because some things just have to be quiet. They sang of the mist-covered hills of home, told Caledonia that they loved her, and sang of ships and of love – always of love. A sailor's farewell to his wrecked ship made them quite sentimental, and then Jim struck up a song about gathering blackberries, and this time Helen didn't join in. Fighting back tears, she listened and didn't say a word. When he finished singing, Jim didn't say anything either. Where had he learnt that song? Helen asked quietly. He'd learnt it from a charming old man at a folk session in Norfolk a few years ago, said Jim, and Helen said that the charming old man was called John Matthews, or at least he'd written the song, and he'd been a friend of her husband's. Had been? asked Jim, and Helen said that her husband had died two years ago and would Jim like anything more to drink, there was still beer in the fridge.

She passed Jim a beer, poured herself a glass of wine, juiced two oranges for the boss, and took the glass to her. Half asleep, the boss mumbled that it was very beautiful, their singing, and she was sure she'd be feeling better tomorrow. Helen checked on Bernard again too and took him another can of Irn-Bru and a few crackers.

When she returned to the kitchen, Jim was singing a song about a bloke in a bowler hat finding fault with a hole, which should be square, not round and not so long, and if it had to be dug at all, it should be somewhere else. It was a very silly song, and that was a good thing, for Helen couldn't have guaranteed what might have happened next otherwise. And Jim couldn't have either.

When the other three returned from the hot tub, Jim was clowning around singing *So be easy and free when you're drinking with me! I'm a man you don't meet every day*, and Helen thought that was quite true; he really was a man you didn't meet every day, although he wasn't at all a show-off like the Jock Stewart in the song. The group from the hot tub were astonished to find a party apparently taking place and quickly went to change into something warm. Mervyn got something to eat after all, and then he went to check on Liz and lay down contentedly next to her bed. He'd had an interesting evening with unexpected encounters.

The investment department manager slept fitfully and kept waking up coughing and wheezing. Helen came in and brought her a honey and lemon and some freshly pressed orange juice. Liz drank, sweated and shivered and went back to sleep. Sometimes she heard singing or laughter coming from the kitchen. It sounded like it came from a long way off.

At some point in the night, she woke to Helen sitting on the edge of her bed. Shivering, Liz swapped her pyjamas, which were soaked in sweat, for a clean nightie she didn't recognise. She didn't care. She didn't care that Helen was there to see her changing either. She took the medicine Helen gave her, she drank because Helen told her to, she didn't stop Helen from sliding a hot water bottle underneath her covers, and then she dozed off again. Hot and sweaty, she tossed and turned, dreaming confused and frightening dreams about birds falling on her head, falling on all of their heads, about bird excrement and feathers. About aggressive birds attacking anything which crossed their path. Enormous, terrifying birds.

At some point, she woke up again, with no idea what time it was. Her head and limbs ached, she was coughing and could hardly breathe through her nose, her mouth was quite dry, and she was utterly exhausted. Helen was there right away, raised a cup of tea to Liz's lips, gave her yet another clean nightie, and dabbed at her face with a damp cloth. Normally, Liz hated being powerless or helpless in any way, but it seemed to do her good to just submit to the care of this cook, who she didn't actually know at all, and to know that things would be better in the morning.

Mervyn, mumbled Liz. She'd given him his food that evening, Helen said, and he'd been outside again too, with the others. He'd woken her up just now, she went on, because he must have noticed Liz wasn't well. Liz tried not to show how moved she was, patted Mervyn briefly on the head, turned away and went straight back to sleep. Mervyn lay back down on the floor beside her bed, and Helen went back to her room. Rachel was sound asleep in their shared double bed. Helen had asked herself whether it had just been down to the nudity in the hot tub that the other three had suddenly seemed like a close-knit circle of friends, intimate and at ease.

The scene repeated itself early the next morning. Mervyn woke Helen, and Helen brought Liz another clean nightie, changed her sheets, gave her some medicine and something to drink – and realised that Liz was on the mend. The boss was shattered but the fever was retreating, her eyes weren't quite as glazed over any more, and she'd soon be doing better. Helen told her she should just sleep for a bit. Thank you, murmured Liz and fell back to sleep.

When everyone was sitting at breakfast the next morning, Helen made up a bit of fruit and toast and took it up to Liz, but she turned out to be fast asleep. That could only be for the best, so Helen returned with the plate to the kitchen, where Jim was standing at the door to the larder with a jar of marmalade in his hand and beaming with joy as he announced to the others that it looked like they'd be eating goose that evening – there was one hanging in the larder, he hadn't even noticed it before! What was she planning to do with it? he asked the startled Helen. Curry, she muttered, she was going to cook a Madras using the vegetables that were left and some fruit. Jim said he'd never heard of goose curry, what an unusual idea, he was intrigued.

Helen hoped her confusion didn't show. So the peacock was now a goose. She glanced at David who was also trying not to give anything away. As far as size was concerned, a goose was of course considerably closer to a peacock than a pheasant was. But Helen had explained to him at length that peacock tasted more like pheasant. Hopefully she hadn't told anyone else there would be pheasant, for she wouldn't be able to get out of this now. So, there was a goose hanging in the larder and nobody seemed to be surprised. David was glad he wasn't in Helen's shoes right now, but he was caught up in this business too, just as much as she was. Helen was above all relieved that she'd already removed the feet and head, and that the bird was plucked.

Andrew was asking himself whether it hadn't been a pheasant that Helen and David had bought at Ryszard's; he thought Helen had mentioned something like that, but he wasn't sure any more. Helen was just as unsure. Had she? When the others were off building the den? She didn't remember and quickly asked after the bump on his head, had it swollen at all overnight, did his head ache? Andrew said he was fine. Talking about his ailments in front of other people embarrassed him a bit, and so he quickly forgot both goose and pheasant.

Luckily, nobody had asked what they'd actually done with the peacock, thought Helen. The boss had just wanted to know it had disappeared completely. The details hadn't interested her.

When Liz next woke – this time from a sound, deep sleep – it was late morning and she did indeed feel considerably better. She sat up. It looked like the sky outside was glorious blue; the gap between the curtains let in a sliver of bright light. She pulled on a thick jumper, popped to the loo, and heard that the others were hashing things out in the sitting room again and clearly enjoying themselves, for she could hear laughter. She was still too weak to be annoyed that she wasn't there with them as she ought to be. She washed her face, avoided looking at herself too closely in the mirror – just in case – and went back to bed.

Five minutes later, Helen came in with a tray of tea and freshly pressed orange juice and warm porridge with honey, cream and fresh fruit. Liz smiled. Helen drew back the curtains and said it was gorgeous weather outside: blue skies and everything looking beautiful, covered with deep snow. And how was Liz feeling? – she looked a lot better. Liz thanked Helen for taking care of her during the night, said she was indeed feeling better, and asked what on earth she was wearing – it was a long time since she'd seen such an old-fashioned nightgown, she said. Helen replied that the nightie belonged to Lady Fiona, who'd dropped by again last night with medicine and hot water bottles and these nightgowns and had asked if there was anything else they needed. Really an exceptionally lovely lady – secretly Helen felt guilty about serving up the McIntoshes' peacock to her crew. But it wasn't her fault it was dead, after all; she was just making the best of the situation. And it wasn't Mervyn's fault either, as the others all thought it was. But whose fault was it? Who had shot the peacock and why? She still had absolutely no idea.

Lady Fiona came into the west wing and asked after the investment department manager. Liz invited her into her room and thanked for her the night-time provision of nightgowns and medicine. The Lady actually had another set of pyjamas with her, the kind for wearing round the house, which Liz – to her own astonishment – gratefully accepted. She was definitely unwell, and just now, loungewear like that was considerably cosier than the serious designer clothing she'd brought with her. It really didn't matter any more – this whole trip was turning out quite differently to how she'd imagined it, these were exceptional circumstances for all of them. Let the men see her in this velour get-up; even Bernard was wearing jeans and a jumper by now, while Jim and David hadn't bothered packing the classic suits they'd wear to the bank in the first place. Andrew managed to be dressed perfectly as always, serious but casual, acceptable in a business setting, and yet at the same time, not unsuitable for this icy, unheatable castle.

The second reason for the Lady's visit was that she'd now received official confirmation that the snowplough wouldn't be coming into the glen today. Which meant that, as expected, the group wouldn't be able to leave today, they didn't have a chance of getting through the snow with their cars. But it was supposed to thaw on Monday and the snowplough would come then too. Ryszard would clear the drive down to the road today, so that tomorrow they'd be able to leave as soon as the snowplough had been. And, of course, they were all welcome to come over to use the McIntoshes' phone to let folk at home and the bank know they'd be staying a day longer.

Liz briefly caught herself thinking she wouldn't have at all minded being snowed in here for a few more days and being looked after by Helen and Lady Fiona. But only very briefly. Of course, she wanted to go home and go to work as usual and take control of her own life again. Home, where she had central heating and a sensible shower. And a chemist around the corner. But she was quite moved by the Lady's care and solicitude. They'd certainly all be glad to take up the offer of using the telephone, she said, and then added, glancing at Helen, that they surely had enough food – maybe they could invite Lord and Lady McIntosh to dinner as a thank you for the wonderful hospitality? She really was very obliged to Lady Fiona, she said. Helen, of course, immediately agreed, but privately she was appalled. This meant she'd have to serve the McIntoshes their own peacock! Lady Fiona said it wasn't at all necessary – she was very sorry herself that they'd been snowed in and couldn't travel home as planned and that the boss had now caught this horrible cold; she rather felt she ought to be the one apologising, to which Liz replied that apologising for the weather was a bit silly. Secretly, Liz felt they really should seriously consider whether they ought to be renting out this unheatable apartment in the depths of winter, but she kept that to herself. She hoped to at least be recovered enough by the evening to join them for dinner.

She was almost regretting the invitation already. Now Helen didn't just have to look after her but also had to cook for two more diners – she'd hardly been thinking straight with her fever brain! Besides, she hadn't discussed it with her colleagues, and who knew what the McIntoshes had been planning to do this evening and whether they were really up for such a spontaneous invitation. Then again, what plans could they have? They were snowed in. Above all, however, Liz felt guilty – her dog had killed the McIntoshes' peacock, after all, and she hadn't told them, and now she was imposing upon them with her illness too. Perhaps she could make up for it with the invitation to dinner.

The Lady was feeling guilty too, because they hadn't told the investment department manager that one of the peacocks had gone crazy and damaged her car.

And, finally, Helen was feeling guilty, because she could hardly serve the McIntoshes their own peacock for dinner! But none of them could back out now. Instead they agreed that the Laird and Lady would join the bankers for dinner that evening, and they all pretended to be delighted. Helen would have liked to have just vanished into thin air. The Lady thought to herself that this would mean she'd have to cook something for Aileen, she couldn't even make herself a sandwich with her arm in plaster.

What took place in the sitting room that morning was astonishing. While Rachel, David and Andrew had been in the hot tub the night before, and Jim had been singing in the kitchen with Helen, Bernard had been in the sitting room, an ice pack on his knee, and had looked over the day's work on the flipcharts and display boards. He'd taken some ideas a step further, added a couple of notes here and there, and re-arranged the self-adhesive organisational charts in a few places. No one had noticed anything that evening. But when they gathered in the sitting room again after breakfast, Bernard cleared his throat and said he'd spontaneously pressed on a little by himself; he hoped they wouldn't hold it against him but he had tried a few things out. It certainly made sense to him, but of course they'd have to wait and see what the boss thought. Of course, the boss, the boss, Andrew muttered, but he saw straight away that Bernard's ideas did indeed make sense. David and Jim quickly realised where Bernard was coming from too. They agreed with him on many points and made even better suggestions for others, and together the four men developed proposals so good that Rachel couldn't help but be amazed. And ask herself what had been going wrong all this time and why they had even needed to book her in the first place! She couldn't add anything conceptually, because the men were already deep in discussions on the intricacies of the financial and banking system. They were so immersed in their subject that all personal animosity seemed forgotten; they debated and developed ideas and plans, and sometimes laughed and would agree with each other and then disagree just as often, and their cheeks got quite flushed. Rachel merely suggested a new methodology now and then or proposed a slightly different approach. She asked herself whether the day would have been like this if they hadn't been snowed in or gone to the hot tub or had a swollen knee or sung together. Or if the boss had been there.

But the boss was in bed in the next room. She would doze off for a bit and then wake up again. She was exhausted but her fever was going down, she no longer had a headache and she was able to breathe much better. And she was getting a cold sore. Luckily, Lady Fiona had brought over some more boxes of tissues – clearly you got into the habit of stockpiling when you lived this far from civilisation. Liz only ever bought one box of tissues at a time.

Whenever she woke up, she could hear lively discussions going on in the sitting room, and they sounded good. She would have liked to be there, at the very least she'd have liked to be a fly on the wall and listen in – the men couldn't just work on without her, perhaps developing ideas she couldn't sign off – but then she was too shattered to be annoyed about it after all and turned over once again. Who knew, maybe her people weren't deciding on any idiotic ideas. Maybe they were even managing without her. Maybe they weren't so stupid at all, and maybe she really was a control freak. But right now, even that didn't bother her, and she fell back to sleep. Helen would come in now and again and ask if she needed anything and how she was doing. And then she took Mervyn out with her and sent him out into the snow with the others.

Rachel and the men barely noticed time pass. After their walk with Mervyn, they ate a quick lunch – a wonderfully thick sweet potato soup with coriander and freshly baked bread – and then got straight back down to business. They realised that they knew surprisingly little about each other's day-to-day work and that they'd make more progress in everything if everyone shared their knowledge and insight. In other words, they needed to talk more and share more with each other. They were all a little shocked at how basic this recognition was. Bernard pointed out that they'd talked a lot more about what they were doing and what they wanted to do next when they'd been building the den. Perhaps because they were doing it for the first time, he added, and didn't have any kind of routine, whereas in the bank everyone always did the same thing and assumed their colleagues knew everything they did. In the woods, none of them had known anything, and they'd therefore been better at collaborating. Jim thought about his finding the gun and not telling anyone about it. He looked at Rachel, but she was acting as if she hadn't noticed. Perhaps she thought nobody had discovered it, thought Jim. Or was it possible she hadn't hidden it there at all? And somebody else had? After all, she hadn't been back to fetch it as far as he was aware. She hadn't gone back into the woods on her own. But who else would hide a gun in the woods and why? That was just silly.

David thought about his keeping from the others that they'd be eating peacock that evening. But that was different, of course. Nobody deliberately concealed anything in the bank; they just didn't communicate enough.

It didn't even occur to Bernard to tell anyone he'd seen the Laird come out of the woods with a shotgun over his shoulder. Why should it?

From time to time, Mervyn left the sitting room to check on his boss, who was generally asleep. Then he paid a visit to Helen in the kitchen, where there was generally a bit of sausage, and returned to the sitting room. He felt quite at home by now. He was content and the humans seemed to be too.

Liz came into the sitting room in the afternoon. She didn't really seem well, but she was nowhere near as ill as she had been and was clearly on the road to recovery. She looked quite ridiculous in the burgundy velour outfit, which no one would have believed she'd wear. And indeed, the very first thing she did was apologise for the outfit and ask them to make allowances, the ensemble had kindly been lent to her by Lady Fiona. She would dress properly for dinner – and by the way, she'd invited the McIntoshes; she'd been a little spontaneous there, she hoped they wouldn't hold it against her. The others seemed to have heard this sentence already today, and they quickly assured her that of course they didn't mind – the McIntoshes really were exceptionally nice people, and they wouldn't accidentally let slip that

Mervyn had their peacock on his conscience. And how was she doing today anyway? Quite well, said Liz, or at any rate much better, Helen had taken wonderful care of her last night. And she'd heard such lively conversations coming from the sitting room all day that she was now quite curious as to what they'd been up to.

The men all agreed that Bernard should present the results. Which he was more than happy to do. He explained how they wanted to concentrate their energy through small changes to their areas of responsibility, specified who would discuss what with whom and when, who was to report to whom, and how they could optimise the communication flow by holding weekly team conferences. That Jim would more or less remain in his galley but was to pay more attention to the others' dietary requirements, and that the control points at which – according to Andrew – the others sat were to be more precisely defined. His colleagues were amazed that he not only made use of the metaphors from their first evening, but completed, added to, and explained them. The boss listened, nodded and was silent. She was so silent that the men almost began to feel uncomfortable, they weren't at all used to this from their boss and wondered whether they'd perhaps gone too far. Here and there, the restructuring proposals did necessarily impact upon the boss's areas of responsibility. They hastened to say that, of course, these were all just suggestions and first drafts, and they were really just thinking out loud.

The boss was silent, however, because she was so impressed. She almost asked herself whether the men perhaps worked better without her. But the atmosphere felt too good for that to be the case. They didn't seem to want to get rid of her, it was more like they were keen to tell her about what they'd achieved. They were all quite focussed on the business at hand. They had considered where people's strengths could best be brought into play and where they could make better use of synergies by working together. They had made sure that everyone would have something new to learn – which they were excited about – and that everyone could let go of something they didn't enjoy, and that overall they would all be more satisfied, herself included, as far as she could make out at this early stage. Maybe she did have quite smart men in her department after all.

Liz quickly realised she was still somewhat under the weather. She thanked them in the strongest terms for the impressive work and said they should take a break sometime too. She was very glad to have such a competent and dedicated team and now she was going back to bed. She'd like to use the bath again before dinner, would that be possible – or did they already have a schedule for the bathroom? David said that technically it was his turn, but he'd far rather use the shower, and the investment department manager actually apologised for having had the ridiculous idea of separating the bathrooms into boys and girls in the first place. She didn't know what she'd been thinking, she said.

Liz got back into bed, nestled down under the covers, looked out into the snowy valley for a moment and then promptly fell asleep. The men were flabbergasted at such positive and emotional words from her.

Over the course of the afternoon, they went over to the McIntoshes one after the other and called home. Jim also made the call to the chair of the board of directors and explained to him that they were snowed in, and that on top of that, Liz was ill and therefore wouldn't be present at the meeting on Monday. The chair was, to put it mildly, not exactly enthusiastic, this was a damn important meeting! But Jim made it clear they didn't have a choice and simply couldn't get out of the valley. And even the chair of the board had no chance against Jim's imperturbable calm. Jim's wife, meanwhile, more or less greeted the news with a shrug. She and Jim were perfectly friendly, but they no longer had much to say to each other.

In contrast, David's husband was evidently disappointed that their day out in Cambridge for his birthday had fallen through, but he soon rallied himself and comforted David, who was just as upset. They assured one another that they'd make up for it another time and that they were looking forward to seeing each other.

Andrew's wife laughed when she heard the story; she could tell her husband was quite relaxed. She was amazed when he told her it was actually all going well and was even quite nice, and she wished him a safe journey home the next day, saying she hoped the snow really would melt by then and the snowplough would arrive. The children sent their love, and his daughter just couldn't wait to show him her medal for gymnastics.

Rachel got in touch with her boss. She could hear the guilt in his voice as he asked how it was going, and she took a certain satisfaction in depicting the weekend's success in the most glowing of terms. She even added that she was downright happy to be able to stay an extra day. And how was he feeling, was he doing better? He was glad it had clearly gone well for her, but he ended the call in a hurry.

Bernard had nobody to call.

That evening there was goose Madras for dinner. David and Helen were the only ones to know there wasn't actually goose Madras for dinner. But, in any case, there was Madras.

The Laird's very first exclamation after greeting everyone in the kitchen was to ask whether someone could please take those peacock feathers outside immediately. It was unlucky to have peacock feathers indoors, everybody knew that – they ought to put them in the wheelie bins outside. He wasn't superstitious, he said, but it was no wonder everyone here was ill and they couldn't leave as planned, what with so many peacock feathers in the flat! The bankers were astonished. Up until now, the Laird had seemed to them quite a sensible man. Helen said she wanted to give the feathers to her nieces and asked if anyone could take them out to her car. The Laird thought that was really quite risky, transporting peacock feathers in a car, you were almost asking for an accident to happen. Helen said she was sure he was right but only if you believed that – and she didn't, so it would be alright. Nobody quite knew what to say.

Jim took the feathers out to Helen's car, and to change the subject, Andrew asked whether someone hadn't said something about pheasant a couple of days ago – it was the season for pheasants, wasn't it? – which the McIntoshes confirmed. Indeed, it was the season for pheasants. The cook showed everyone to their places as if she hadn't heard the question. Everyone sat down and then Helen had them pass her their plates for her to serve up the curry, while David concentrated on making sure everyone had something to drink. Jim said he'd read somewhere that pheasants were specially reared and then set out here in the valleys so that they could be shot. The Laird said that was right, that was what happened, particularly with grouse. Really he found the whole business ludicrous – just so a few city folk could come here and indulge their passion for the shoot! But he permitted it on his estate all the same, for that was just the way things were. The time when the young birds were set out was always so ridiculous, because they didn't know life in the wild at all. They'd wander around on the roads in groups and were too daft to flee into the bushes when a car approached, they generally ran along the road in front of the car instead, sometimes for hundreds of yards until you'd expect them to collapse from exhaustion. But at some point, they normally did manage to flutter away. After a few days, the birds would then acclimatise and spread out across the land a bit more and you could drive along the roads again. At least until the shooting parties arrived, that was a whole other kettle of fish. The whole thing really was messed up in a way, said the Lady, but of course it was nice for them too, as they were always given a pheasant or two and sometimes even some game as a gift from the shooting parties. The men were silent because their boss was, of course, one of the very people who only ventured into the countryside for the shoot. To their surprise, Liz outed herself, saying she probably ought to confess – she was one of those game shooters from the city herself.

The McIntoshes hurriedly said it wasn't the individuals that were the problem but the system. The boss smiled and said, yes – but the system consisted of individuals and, as such, she would have to ask herself whether it was all so good and proper after all.

Lady Fiona changed the subject and asked about the recipe for this sensational curry. It tasted quite particular somehow; she probably wouldn't even have realised it was goose, she said, how was it seasoned? Helen told them a bit about spice mixes and said that in India every cook with an ounce of pride had their own mixture, as was the case with good Indian restaurants in Britain too. This here was a Madras mixture, a somewhat spicier curry powder with more chilli in it, and, of course, it also contained turmeric, cumin, coriander, pepper and fenugreek – as all curries do, actually. She explained a lot about spice mixes and the traditions of Indian seasoning, lost herself in the details of the origins of turmeric and its relationship with ginger, got onto the cultivation of cumin and chilli, and talked – as she always did when she was nervous – far too much. At the back of her mind, she was above all afraid someone would bite on some lead shot. How would shot have got into a goose? She had picked it out meticulously, thinking the whole time how much more plausible the claim that they were eating pheasant would have been, for a goose would have been properly slaughtered, not shot. She could only hope she really had got it all out, but that wasn't particularly likely.

Luckily, her chatter didn't bother anyone, as most of those present were preoccupied with their own guilty consciences anyway. Hamish and Fiona because their peacock had damaged the investment department manager's car and they had kept this from her; the manager herself, along with Rachel and the men, because they thought Mervyn had killed the McIntoshes' peacock; and Helen and David because the goose wasn't a goose but was actually the peacock, and so the two of them were deceiving all of the others – the McIntoshes, the boss, David's colleagues, Rachel.

Helen chatted on for a good bit longer, all the while desperately trying to change the subject so nobody would get onto talking about the taste of the meat. Instead, she asked the group whether any of them had ever been to India.

Liz had indeed been to India for work. She was rather quiet this evening though, for she was still far from well. She had quite a blocked nose and was mainly focussing on not chewing with her mouth open while still managing to breathe. She didn't eat much, and really she would have liked to just crawl back into bed, but she was making a valiant effort. She was looking flawless again in designer jeans and a cashmere jumper, simultaneously elegant and casual – neither as formal as she was in the bank nor anything like as intimate and vulnerable as she'd looked earlier in the Lady's house clothes. She only talked a little about India and said that above all she'd really enjoyed the food there, which didn't exactly help Helen in her attempt to change the subject.

The Lady said she had only had a curry this delicious once before: last summer. There had been a charming couple here, also from London, who had cooked a wonderful meal for them. Under no circumstances did the Laird want the conversation to go in the direction of what else had happened that same evening, and so he joked that people always assumed it was so lonely up here that you'd always want to travel, but the opposite was true – you just had to stay at home and the world would come to you. The most delicious Indian meal in the world was to be had on a snowy evening in a deserted glen in Scotland! The Lady laughed at him and said, oh aye, this old armchair traveller! She herself would love to travel through Asia one day, but it was very hard to get her husband to leave the glen. He'd always use the animals and the estate generally as an excuse, as if Aileen and Ryszard couldn't manage on their own for a few weeks. Of course they could, said the Laird, and he wasn't all that bad – they did go away sometimes, last year to Rome for example. And with that, they had finally managed to change the subject. From Italy, they moved onto Greece and then to Turkey; they talked about holidays, study trips and friends who had emigrated, and they gradually began to relax.

Until the Laird said, apropos goose – had anyone seen the goose? Their goose, that was, the one which was always wandering around outside and scolding people. He'd last seen her yesterday morning sometime, and today she hadn't shown up at all. Which was strange, because normally when there was this much snow, she would go to the shed behind the house and fight over food with the peacocks. No, the bankers said after thinking about it, they hadn't seen the goose today, although they'd been outside twice – but then they hadn't been keeping an eye out for it either. Nobody had noticed that they hadn't encountered the goose at all.

Andrew froze. Last night, Mervyn had disappeared for a while when they had been sitting in the hot tub and had illicitly let him off his lead. And if Mervyn had killed a peacock on the first day, then perhaps he had the goose on his conscience too and had dragged its remains who knew where. And in the end, maybe he'd brought them to the cook, and she'd made the best of things. Perhaps he ought to look tomorrow morning and see whether Mervyn's tracks were still visible in the snow, but they had probably disappeared a while ago. David and Rachel went pale too. Nobody wanted to have done that to the McIntoshes, first their peacock, now maybe their goose – what sort of feathered massacre was this? Mervyn had never seemed like this before, he came across as quite gentle and obedient really. A setter wasn't exactly a wolf.

Helen laughed awkwardly and hurriedly said that the goose on their plates, at least, was one she'd brought with her, it had lived a happy life on a meadow at a farm near hers. David choked. He didn't know whether he should be impressed or appalled by how naturally and convincingly Helen could lie. Heavens above, the Lady said, of course they hadn't thought for a second that this was their goose! – why would they? The curried goose had just reminded the Laird he'd wanted to ask whether anyone had seen it. Anyway, their goose was already very old, she certainly wouldn't taste this tender, she must be as tough as leather by now.

David fell silent again. He thought the peacock tasted very good, but he wouldn't have noticed any more than the others that it wasn't goose he was eating. The dish was so well seasoned that you really couldn't tell what the meat was. Or could you? He didn't care. He felt bad, because he knew it was the McIntoshes' peacock they were eating, and only he and Helen were aware of this and they were deceiving the others. None of which changed the fact that the McIntoshes had lost their goose and Mervyn had disappeared for a while yesterday evening. Who knew what he'd done to the bird or whether he'd even polished it off? – maybe the McIntoshes would find its feathers and remains in a few days' time. If Mervyn really did have the goose on his conscience, then David was now complicit on two counts. He felt quite wretched.

Luckily, the boss changed the subject this time and told the McIntoshes about the damage to her car, which she couldn't understand. She thought it must have happened on the way into the valley, did that often happen here? She wasn't used to driving on such rural roads herself. The McIntoshes put on their best show of surprise. Rachel half expected them to say that one of the peacocks sometimes attacked blue objects, but they didn't. On the whole, the change of subject didn't exactly contribute to relaxing the situation.

And so the evening passed in a peculiar atmosphere. They all felt guilty for different reasons, they all would have liked to set things right, they were all being friendly and making an effort. The investment department manager left very early for bed, apologising profusely for doing so. She still wasn't exactly well, she said. It had been a lovely evening but she urgently needed to be horizontal again, she really was very sorry. The others shouldn't feel like they needed to leave too, they were welcome to carry on as they were.

Which Lord and Lady McIntosh of course didn't do, departing shortly afterwards too. They said thank you for the delicious goose curry and that they would come by the next day and let the bankers know as soon as they'd had the news that the snow-plough had been and they could leave. They could expect this to be early afternoon, it certainly wouldn't be first thing. They apologised once again for the circumstances and for the group being snowed in, and the bankers insisted once again that the McIntoshes weren't to blame, quite the contrary, they had even warned them this would happen, so it really was their own fault. They thanked the McIntoshes in return for the hospitality, particularly for the use of the hot tub and for the Lady being so straightforward and obliging when attending to the needs of their boss the night before.

On leaving the west wing, Hamish and Fiona McIntosh took another turn around the house to look for the goose. They even went to the washhouse where the goose always tended to linger, but she wasn't there either. They checked all of the places the goose normally hung around. At one point, they briefly thought they heard her gobbling – but it was probably some other noise after all.

That really was a tasty curry, Hamish said, and Fiona replied, yes, it certainly was. After a pause, she added that their goose would never have been so tender, she was ancient – that really couldn't have been her. The Laird said he hadn't meant to imply that, of course he wouldn't accuse any of the bankers of something like that and certainly not the cook. Lady Fiona, however, said if she were to believe anyone capable of something like that it would be this cook, she got the impression the woman was a canny one. But not so canny she'd slaughter her hosts' goose – surely not, said Hamish. It was much more probable that the goose had just died somewhere in the bushes, he said. Perhaps her time had simply come. Or she'd frozen to death – although it had certainly been considerably colder for longer than this the past few winters. Or a fox or a wildcat had got her. That was probably most likely. They didn't get many wildcats around here any more, but it did happen occasionally.

Hamish asked whether geese grew forgetful when they got older too and whether she could have just got lost, but neither of them were really in the mood to laugh. Victoria hadn't been dead all that long, then Hamish had had to shoot the crazy peacock, and now the goose had disappeared. It really was enough now, they thought, all remaining animals were to stay healthy and happy and present, thank you very much! They were glad to be greeted joyfully by Albert and Britney as they entered the back door to the kitchen after taking another turn around the house. They had agreed not to tell Aileen they thought the goose was missing.

Aileen, however, had been out with the dogs several times that day, and she had also noticed the goose was missing. She was now able to wriggle into her jacket and slip into her boots all by herself. And to coincidentally bump into Ryszard when she was out. While the McIntoshes were in the west wing, she had been outside with Albert and Britney again and had taken another look to see whether the goose had turned up. At first, she hadn't wanted to worry the McIntoshes, but now she'd decided to tell them. When the two of them came into the kitchen, she first asked what the meal had been like and what they had eaten. Curry, said the Laird cautiously, and Aileen immediately asked what kind of curry. Goose, said Lady Fiona, which was very unusual for a curry but it tasted excellent – the cook really knew her stuff and had told them all kinds of interesting facts about curry. Fiona McIntosh was trying to distract Aileen from the subject of geese, but Aileen was worried. And she said so. She hadn't seen the goose all day, she said, she wasn't with the peacocks in the shed. Had either of them seen her? Now that she thought about it, she had last seen her sometime yesterday afternoon.

Lord McIntosh frowned and said, she wasn't suggesting that Helen would – Ach no! said Aileen, she hadn't even thought of that, she'd just been worrying about the goose. Although now the Laird mentioned it, that cook did come across as very determined, and she had needed to cook for a day longer than planned.

Oh please, said Fiona McIntosh, that was just absurd! And she repeated the discussion she and the Laird had had.

Aileen asked if she should go out again and look for the goose. The McIntoshes waved the offer aside, they'd just done that. The goose still wasn't in the shed, and they had already walked around the house twice and had looked everywhere where the goose normally liked to spend her time.

And so they made themselves a last cup of tea and had an early night. If they had gone out again, they would have seen three figures in bathrobes – but no dog – traipsing through the snow towards the hot tub.

The group of three in the hot tub were fairly quiet. Until at some point Rachel said softly – Mervyn surely didn't kill the goose though, did he? Andrew and David couldn't quite picture it either, but Mervyn had killed the peacock, after all. Had they noticed the peacock was remarkably undamaged? asked Andrew. A dog wouldn't normally be that careful when killing an animal and it wouldn't normally take it to its mistress either. Maybe it had something to do with the fact that Mervyn wasn't a wild animal, said David, and was used to the city instead – who knew what that did to a dog's instincts? Or maybe it had something to do with him going on shoots with the boss but only retrieving animals which had been shot, not ones he'd killed himself. It was all very peculiar, they thought, and Rachel wondered aloud whether Mervyn could have taken the goose to somebody too, namely to the cook. She was spoiling him rotten after all. A dog which gave his mistress a peacock might perhaps also give the cook a goose. Maybe Mervyn wasn't as harmless as he appeared. Rachel and Andrew both concluded that it was at least possible they had just eaten the McIntoshes' goose.

David, of course, knew they hadn't eaten this goose or any other goose but rather had eaten the peacock. That didn't explain what Mervyn had done with the goose though. If he had anything to do with its disappearance, that is, which was indeed more than possible.

He was feeling more and more uncomfortable. That was going too far, he said. Helen wouldn't ever do something like that! Which was yet another lie. That was exactly what Helen had done, just not to the goose. David was on the point of telling the others everything. Rachel said Helen hadn't been in bed half the time last night. She'd assumed Helen was looking after Liz and taking her drinks and medicine and clean nighties and checking her temperature, but maybe she'd also used the time to pluck the goose and get it ready to cook. The men asked whether she honestly believed Helen would do something like that, and Rachel hurriedly said, oh no, that was just a joke, although she admitted it wasn't a very funny one – of course they hadn't eaten the goose!

David was silent. And so Rachel and Andrew fell silent too, but it was a different kind of silence to the one the night before. All three of them were asking themselves whether Mervyn could have killed the goose, and two of them thought it possible that Helen had prepared the goose overnight and that they'd just eaten it. All three of them wished for last night's atmosphere back again, but even silence couldn't recreate it.

Gradually the warm water took its effect though, as did the stars and the snow, which reflected the moonlight. Andrew was looking forward to seeing his wife, David to seeing his husband, and Rachel was glad the weekend had been quite successful in the end. Of the activities she'd planned, they had only started on the den. She hadn't even suggested any of the other activities because they couldn't go outside, and anyway, the bankers worked in quite a different way to what she'd imagined. As it was, she had just intervened occasionally to facilitate discussion, and the programme she'd planned had gone out the window. She wasn't sure whether her presence had been of any use to the group, but right now she didn't care. The weekend had certainly been worthwhile for the group itself – you could tell that just by looking at them, and it was also clear from the results on the display boards. It didn't really matter to what extent she'd played a part in that, at least not to the bank. But perhaps it did to her. She slid a bit deeper into the water.

An almost childish glee was suddenly growing in David at having been a part of such a daring prank. He hadn't hurt anyone, after all; the peacock was already dead, and it hadn't been his idea to cook it. He was astonished at himself for feeling this way and just hoped it wouldn't turn out that Mervyn really had killed the goose. They should have just kept him on the lead.

There was no singing when they returned to the house this time. The boss was getting a good night's sleep. Bernard was already in bed too – they had swapped; David was sleeping in the top bunk now because Bernard couldn't make it up the ladder with his swollen knee – and Jim and Helen were sitting in the kitchen with a glass of wine. The other three joined them for a little while, but the conversation didn't really get off the ground.

The next morning the situation was as follows: Lord McIntosh knew the peacock had damaged the investment department manager's car, and he had therefore shot the peacock and left the body in the woods. He had told Ryszard, as this meant he didn't have to lure the peacocks into the woods three times a day and keep them away from the house and could instead devote himself to more important things. Lady Fiona was, of course, also in the know. They still hadn't told Aileen.

If Ryszard had looked more closely, he would have noticed a large bird hanging in the larder. He hadn't paid it any attention though and he might have taken the bird to be a goose. Or maybe not.

The visitors knew Mervyn had killed a peacock and thought David had disposed of it in the woods with Helen's help. David and Helen knew they had done no such thing but had instead served up the dead peacock in the Madras which the team had eaten. Only Helen knew Mervyn hadn't killed the bird in the first place and it had actually been shot. With lead. She couldn't make head nor tail of why someone would do something like that though. She suspected someone had been poaching and had almost been caught at the last minute and so had left the dead peacock in the woods. A gourmet poacher, evidently. Anyone else would have simply shot a pheasant.

Above all, she was glad to have survived the evening with the peacock Madras. Perhaps one or two people harboured the suspicion they had eaten the McIntoshes' goose – but that was just utterly absurd, and it would all be cleared up as soon as the goose turned up again. Which of course it would. The group probably wouldn't hear about it though; after all, the snowplough was meant to come today, and they would return to London. The question of the goose's whereabouts remained.

David knew they had eaten the peacock and he was jointly responsible for the fact that Mervyn had at the very least had the opportunity to kill the goose. He still couldn't quite imagine Mervyn doing so, but he had clearly killed the peacock. The question of the goose's whereabouts remained.

They all knew the boss's car had been damaged. On their arrival, Rachel had seen one of the peacocks tearing a sheet of blue tissue paper to shreds, and she suspected this peacock had also damaged the boss's car. She could hardly voice that thought though – it would have sounded like she was accusing the McIntoshes, who really weren't to blame. She had watched the peacocks very closely in the days which followed, because given her blue jacket, she was a little scared of them. But she hadn't noticed any other unusual behaviour. Perhaps the very peacock Mervyn had killed was the crazy one – its instincts were clearly somewhat muddled, perhaps that was why it hadn't managed to escape from the dog in time. Otherwise it surely would have just fluttered up into the nearest tree.

As far as the goose was concerned, Rachel wasn't quite sure what to think. She could certainly imagine Helen plucking and cooking a goose which was already dead. But if a dog had killed a bird, it definitely wouldn't bring it into the kitchen undamaged, and she couldn't believe Helen had served them Mervyn's leftovers. Besides, the McIntoshes' goose was old. It surely wouldn't have been as tasty and tender as the meat they'd eaten. The question of the goose's whereabouts remained.

Jim knew a gun had been hidden in the woods, not far from the spot where Mervyn had killed the peacock, but he'd thought it had been part of some little facilitation game. Still, he couldn't figure out how Rachel had smuggled it out there or when she'd fetched it back and where it was now. She must have secretly slipped out again at night.

When eating the goose curry, he'd bitten down on lead shot. The McIntoshes' goose had disappeared. It was obvious what had happened, even if he didn't understand why Helen had done it. Geese weren't normally shot but slaughtered properly. Who had hidden the gun in the woods? Rachel? Could Helen have found it there? And shot the goose with it? The two women were probably in cahoots. There was no doubt in Jim's mind that they had eaten the McIntoshes' goose and that it had been shot with the gun he'd seen in the woods. There had been absolutely no need for such a brazen coup – they'd had ample food for everyone. But he found he had to admire Helen's audacity. Whatever her reason for doing it. Perhaps she'd simply felt like eating goose.

Bernard could have told him who the gun belonged to and who had fetched it out of the woods, as he had seen the Laird coming home with it. However, he didn't know that the Laird had gone into the woods without a gun that evening and that the gun had been there just as long as the dead peacock. He didn't consider it particularly noteworthy anyway. The Laird was a landowner with woods on his estate after all, presumably that sometimes involved wandering around with a gun.

What was far more important was that his knee was doing a lot better this morning. He was generally feeling surprisingly well, he'd almost whistled a tune on his way to the bathroom. The question of the goose's whereabouts remained – but if he was honest it didn't particularly interest him. Animals which roam around freely disappear sometimes. Or maybe it had frozen to death.

Andrew somehow had it in his head that somebody had mentioned pheasant. He had been a little surprised when they'd then eaten a goose which Helen had brought with her – although he hadn't noticed a goose when carrying in the provisions. But perhaps that didn't mean anything. And perhaps he'd only imagined the thing about the pheasant. The question of the goose's whereabouts remained. Mervyn had had the opportunity to kill it, and they had eaten a goose. He'd rather not know precisely what that meant.

Liz was also feeling considerably better. She was able to breathe more easily and, while she was still rather exhausted, she somehow felt rested at the same time. And she was hungry.

The boss knew even less than the rest of them about either the peacock or the goose. She didn't draw any kind of conclusion from the fact that they'd eaten a goose and a goose had disappeared. She was surprised Mervyn had killed a peacock and wondered what had got into him. And what had happened to her car. There was also the question of what had happened to the McIntoshes' goose.

Mervyn was the only one who knew what had happened to the goose, but nobody asked him. Otherwise, Mervyn didn't understand very much. He had retrieved the shot bird the way he had been taught, and he had been scolded. First the humans had left the bird in the woods and then they had fetched it, naked, into the house after all. That was curious. He also didn't understand why he had to constantly be on a lead when there was so much to explore, nor why he wasn't allowed to run around with the other dogs, and what his boss had against the stuffed monkey which smelt so good.

They were all glad they'd made such good progress with the teambuilding.

After breakfast they all went out for a walk together. Even Bernard joined them, saying his knee was already feeling much better, and so did Liz, who thought it was time for a little fresh air. The boss had announced they weren't going to do any more work today. They had achieved enough, much more than she'd expected they would that weekend. Today they weren't going to do anything other than drive home – the journey would be long enough. Everything else could wait until tomorrow.

As they walked, they made subdued jokes to the effect that Mervyn hopefully wasn't about to fetch the dead goose from the woods, but nobody could really laugh about it. Besides, Mervyn was on his lead. When they passed the spot where he'd carried the peacock out of the undergrowth, Liz looked him deep in the eyes and said she still couldn't believe it. Mervyn looked up at her but didn't understand what she wanted from him. His mistress had been rather odd lately.

A few steps behind them, Bernard and David were thinking back to the same incident. Bernard wondered at the fact that Mervyn had killed a bird but not eaten it and asked himself whether peacocks maybe didn't taste particularly good. He said to David, really they could have eaten the peacock, given that Mervyn had already butchered it – it had almost been a waste to bury it. Did David know whether you could eat peacocks? No idea, said David, he'd certainly never heard of people eating peacock, and then he was ashamed. Why not? asked Bernard. You could eat other birds that size – geese and turkeys, for example. Although peacocks must have less fat on them than geese – and then it occurred to him that the curry last night hadn't seemed overly fatty at all. But he didn't say that out loud and then the thought was gone.

After the walk, everyone packed their things. They all felt almost melancholy. It was beautiful up here with the snow and all the animals and the rushing stream and the hot tub and the McIntoshes, who were charming. And it was so far away from the rest of the world.

Liz went into the kitchen to ask Helen for a final mug of honey and lemon. On the way, she noticed that one of the pictures on the wall was askew and she straightened it. The print was called *The Weighing of the Birds* and showed a party returning from a shoot, placing various birds on a large set of scales: pheasants, partridges, grouse – there was even a swan. Really, she said to Helen, they could well have eaten the peacock, given that it was already dead. Did Helen know whether you could eat peacock? Helen kept her cool. But of course, she said, you could cook them beautifully with lemon and basil, for example, or roast them whole, you just had to wrap them in enough bacon so they didn't get too dry. To be honest, she added, she had briefly thought about it but hadn't dared to suggest it to Liz. Oh dear! said Liz. Did she really seem so terrifying that you couldn't make any unusual suggestions around her? Not any more, said Helen and smiled. Liz took the mug and went back to her room to pack her suitcase.

Helen fetched the Tupperware with the peacock liver from the fridge and packed it right at the bottom of the box of food. She would take it home and make a lovely pâté with it. And she'd serve it to someone who would be sure to appreciate it.

The snowplough came at around midday, and the driver said it shouldn't be a problem to get into the glen with normal cars any more. They should just be careful at this one steep bit, it was a northerly slope and could often be a bit slippy. The McIntoshes bid their guests farewell and apologised for the inconveniences, and the guests said not at all, they were grateful for the wonderful hospitality. Liz, in particular, thanked them for being so obliging and helpful on the night of her fever, and so the London bankers departed amid a mutual exchange of courtesies.

Getting into her car, Liz noticed the damage again and was puzzled once more. Well, there was nothing to be done about it, the repairs would hardly cost the earth. There were more important things.

Hamish and Fiona McIntosh were jolly glad the bankers were gone. So glad that they impulsively opened a bottle of prosecco and burst into peals of laughter. First the peacock had wrecked the stuck-up cow's car, then the Laird had shot the peacock (which wasn't a laughing matter at all), then the bankers had been snowed in and had to stay a day longer, then the stuck-up cow had fallen ill and suddenly wasn't such a stuck-up cow after all, then the fuse had burnt through and finally the goose had disappeared too. That was a wee bit too much for just one weekend. And they still weren't quite certain they hadn't eaten their own goose. That cook really was a lovely person, but she was also very capable; they agreed they'd trust her to know how to slaughter a goose but couldn't imagine her stealing theirs. Why would she? But a tiny doubt remained.

Aileen, however, was convinced the McIntoshes had eaten the goose. What other explanation was there? – a goose couldn't just disappear like that. The goose had never disappeared before, she had lived here for ages and was always to be found within the same radius. And where was the cook meant to have got the goose she'd cooked? Certainly not from Ryszard – he didn't sell geese. Had she brought it with her? That's what she'd told them over dinner, the McIntoshes explained, but Aileen wasn't buying it. No, there was no doubt in Aileen's mind: the McIntoshes had eaten their own goose.

Later in the afternoon the Laird and Lady went for a walk, taking Albert with them. Their minds were still on the group of bankers, yesterday's dinner and the goose. They went for a long walk through the grounds, and neither of them was particularly talkative until the Lady quietly started to talk about Aileen's broken arm; she'd have to wear the plaster for four more weeks, so would have stay with them until shortly before Christmas, and Fiona really could have done without that. If Aileen were in a position to help her in any way, then of course it would be different, but at the moment, she was no help and an additional burden.

Fiona and Hamish considered how they were going to manage the next few weeks. Christmas was fast approaching and with it the arrival of their children, the semester was coming to an end, Hamish would have his students' essays and exams to mark, and Fiona had the annual accounts to do. As they kept thinking of more and more items needing dealt with in December, they didn't notice Albert stopping at the ice house, looking in the window and barking. They carried on walking and only noticed his absence after a while. They called him. Albert didn't show up. They called him again and then called more loudly. Albert remained wherever he was. They could hear him barking in the distance.

The Laird retraced his steps and called once more. Albert appeared at the end of the path and barked. Then he looked at the Laird, barked again, turned around and trotted back to where he'd been – until eventually the Laird understood that Albert wanted to show him something.

Albert ran to the ice house. Every few steps, he'd stop to make sure the Laird was still following him. A short distance behind the Laird came the Lady. Shortly before the ice house, there was another small power struggle between Albert and Lord McIntosh. But the Laird had to understand there was something here which wasn't right! Albert didn't understand the goose's language, but he knew the goose didn't normally sound like this. He also knew she never normally went in here. He had to keep his herd together, and the goose belonged to the herd and not in this cold, dark hole.

At some point, the Laird finally condescended to walk towards the ice house window. He slipped, fell down and swore. And then he was there.

The goose was sitting in the ice house. She had tumbled in around midday on Saturday and had been there ever since. She would never have dared to go in of her own volition, it was down a steep slope and it was dark. But with the first snow on the ground, the goose had tried to take a shortcut around the house and had slipped – and as she was then down by the entrance to the ice house and couldn't get back up the bank because of the snow, she had stared into the ice house for a while because she was scared. Her eyes had got used to the dark and eventually she had waddled inside. And discovered it was somewhat warmer in here than it was outside, and there was also some hay. The Laird had stored the hay there because it stayed nice and dry in the ice house. Hay wasn't exactly the goose's favourite food but it was better than nothing, and besides, it kept you warm. And so she had been stuck in here for two days.

It wasn't as if no one had known she was there – two of the peacocks knew and Mervyn did too. They had all looked through the small opening at the back, and the goose had gobbled at them. But still nobody had come to fetch her out.

The Laird called to his wife, here she was! And his wife asked, here who was? The goose, of course, called Hamish, and considered how best to get her out of there. You could go into the ice house when there was no snow – after all, he'd stored some hay there in late summer – but right now it was difficult, it was down a steep dyke and the entrance was full of snow. Besides, he assumed the goose had slid down the dyke and couldn't get up again on her own, otherwise she wouldn't have stayed in there for days. So he couldn't simply shoo her out and up, and from experience he knew she wouldn't let anyone touch her, so he'd have to build her some kind of pathway. They needed a ramp.

Hamish praised Albert effusively for his really quite extraordinary intelligence, thanked him for finding the goose and leading him there, and then they went home and phoned Ryszard.

Ryszard came and brought a few long planks with him, which they used to build a ramp for the goose. The goose was a little daft and a little scared and besides, she had been sitting in the dark for days and had only had a bit of hay to eat, so it took a while before she understood what she was supposed to do and made her way across the planks and out into the open. Once outside she didn't gobble, and she didn't assault anyone, and she didn't flap her wings. Making no further commentary, she merely waddled straight ahead, making as fast a bee line as she could for the feeding station in the shed.

Hamish and Ryszard just left the planks where they were and went back to the kitchen, where the Lady made them each a hot toddy. She poured honey, whisky and freshly squeezed lemon juice into glasses and filled them up with hot tea. The men declared their love for her on the spot, for they were both thoroughly frozen through. They'd slipped and fallen in the snow and had worked on with wet trousers. That numpty of a goose, they told the Lady, first of all she hadn't understood, and then she hadn't even thanked them!

And to think that they might have eaten her! said the Lady. The goose ought to be grateful they hadn't – and that Albert had found her in the ice house. Ungrateful creature! She told Ryszard of their suspicion that they might have eaten the goose, and Ryszard said surely no one would behave like that, and certainly not that nice lady who had known so much about vegetables.

Aileen was very glad the goose was back and hadn't been eaten. Everyone was relieved – until Aileen said she didn't want to worry the McIntoshes again, but she thought one of the peacocks might be missing too. There ought to be another male, a fairly young one, maybe the one which had occasionally acted crazy over the summer. Incidentally, she had noticed the left wing of the bank manager's blue car had been dented and scratched at the back. She looked expectantly from the Laird to the Lady and back again. The phone rang. The Lady answered it, the Laird busied himself at the stove, and Ryszard started playing with Britney.

It was the Bakshis, calling as they'd said they would. They wanted to come up over New Year, asked whether the cottage was free and had sufficient heating, and were delighted when the Lady immediately invited them to her Hogmanay party, which was always great fun. Then they asked how the peacock was doing and whether it had calmed down. Lady Fiona glanced at Aileen, who already suspected something anyway, took a deep breath and said to the Bakshis, well actually, it was like this, and said to Aileen, she should listen too – she wouldn't like it and Fiona was very sorry, but the Laird had had to shoot the peacock. She explained what had happened and that the Laird hadn't had a choice at the time. Mrs Bakshi offered her condolences and cautiously asked how much it had upset the McIntoshes.

It upset Aileen, at least, very much indeed. She said quietly, her lower lip trembling, that she didn't think it was right, and then she was silent because the Lady was still on the phone. Aileen suddenly felt quite miserable. The Laird had shot a peacock just because it had been a wee bit mental, she'd been stuck here for days and couldn't do anything at all except go out for walks, her arm was really itchy under her plaster, and she had no idea how she'd be spending Christmas. She swallowed, and then someone was standing behind her – a hand rested on her shoulder, a large calloused hand with dirt under its fingernails, and squeezed it gently. Just briefly, then Ryszard had gone past, but it was long enough for Aileen to fear she might burst into tears altogether. Very quickly, she picked up her jacket and went out. She took Britney and Albert with her. Ryszard followed her after exchanging a look with the Laird, while the Lady finished her conversation with the Bakshis.

And then Lord and Lady McIntosh sat at the kitchen table, stirred their drinks, and asked themselves how on earth people lit on the idea that nothing ever happened in such a deserted glen. They were sorry about the peacock, and they were also sorry they'd kept it from Aileen and then had had to tell her after all. But at least the goose had turned up again, and they'd survived the invasion of the bankers. Life went on.

For the peacock, of course, life didn't go on, and so Aileen insisted – when she came back in with noticeably reddened cheeks – that he should at least have a proper burial. That was the least they could do, she said, and she made no secret of what she thought of the Laird simply shooting him. They could have shut him in the ice house for a spell and then asked the vet for advice, she said, and Hamish had to concede that she was right. With all this snow he wasn't sure he'd find the dead peacock again though, and besides, the ground was frozen, so they wouldn't easily be able to dig a grave. Couldn't they simply leave him in the woods? – the woods made a nice grave after all. Hamish was exhausted from the bankers' visit and all this snow, he just wanted to sit down in front of the fire and read. Aileen gave him a look which brooked no refusal and said Ryszard could dig a grave with the small digger he used to dig ditches, he wouldn't have to shovel it by hand.

Come on then, said Fiona. And so Lord and Lady McIntosh stood up, put on their warm jackets, took a basket and went into the woods to fetch the dead peacock.

Shortly before Christmas, Helen's old friend Indira visited her in her small London flat. They hadn't seen one another for a few months and had a whole lot to catch up on. They'd just be having a simple sandwich, said Helen, a glint in her eye. Indira knew very well what that meant. Helen served up wine and homemade bread, and then came the surprise; she'd made a liver pâté. Indira was to guess what kind of animal it was from, she said, and with that it was clear it wasn't any of the usual ones. Definitely bird, Indira could taste that. Perhaps pheasant, but there was something unusual about it. It surely couldn't be peacock liver? Yes, said Helen, that was exactly what it was. And then she told the whole story: how she'd been booked by a London private bank's investment department for a teambuilding exercise somewhere in Scotland, in a small valley at the foot of the Highlands, and how the investment department manager's dog had killed a peacock, and a young banker had been told to dispose of the body. And how she'd lent this banker, David, a helping hand and had done the obvious thing and prepared the peacock for the pot – it would have been a waste to just leave the bird to rot in the woods when it was already dead. Of course, she couldn't have told the boss what they were doing. Indira nodded, astonished, and Helen chattered on as was her way. While plucking the bird, she'd realised the manager's dog hadn't killed the peacock at all, but that it had been shot – although she couldn't figure out why anyone would shoot a peacock and then leave it lying in the woods. Presumably someone had wanted to do some poaching and had been disturbed – but at any rate, she had cooked the peacock in a curry and hadn't told the bankers. Or at least only David, a charming young man – but he still thought Mervyn, the dog, had killed the peacock. She did feel rather guilty now, particularly because the boss had then invited their hosts – who were extremely pleasant and friendly – to dinner, and so she had served Lord and Lady McIntosh their own peacock! But she really couldn't have known that would happen. And by that point, it was of course far too late to tell anyone they hadn't got rid of the peacock as instructed. In the end, she'd had to claim the peacock was goose, even though goose tastes totally different and is much more fatty, but no one had suspected a thing. How did she find the pâté?

Helen was so engrossed in her tale that she didn't even notice as her friend's jaw dropped.

Oh, the pâté... Very good, said Indira Bakshi. The pâté was outstanding.

Translator's Note

Explaining the set-up of *The Peacock* to friends has prompted a surprising number of bewildered responses: 'So, you're translating it into... which language?' The idea of a German book set in Scotland and translated 'back' into English was clearly a novel one.

And it did spark some interesting translation questions. The question of exoticisation versus localisation is a favourite – if rather tired – topic of translation seminars: do you try and preserve the 'foreignness' of a text or do you transpose the cultural references to something the reader will know? (Do your characters eat Germany's omnipresent paprika crisps, or do they buy a packet of salt and vinegar?) With *The Peacock*, I found myself working the other way round. On the whole, the Scotland Isabel evokes is an extremely familiar one. The various higgledy-piggledy buildings turned into tourist accommodation – complete with slanting floors and wonky sinks – had me laughing in recognition. But there were moments when I felt Germanness had slipped in accidentally: when hot drinks which most certainly weren't tea were referred to as such, or when Rachel told Helen, the cook, that the group would take a packed lunch and instead eat a bigger meal in the evening – as if lunch were the main meal of the day, as it is Germany. On the whole, I found myself softening these moments. I wanted British readers to sink into the book as comfortably as I had, without anything to jolt them out of that experience.

Then there was the question of dialects. Most of the novel is in indirect speech, with characters from London, 'the foot of the Highlands' and Poland, and with a whole range of ages and class backgrounds. Getting the different voices right was key to translating the novel – although the indirect speech meant I was able to soften Aileen's broader Scots into Scots English (English syntax and grammar, but with Scots dialect words) for the sake of continuity.

We think about dialects as being about the catchphrases, all *Haud Yer Wheesht*s and *Wae'aye*s. But as any child in an unfamiliar playground can tell you, it's as much about whether you say living or sitting room, and whether you're going home for your tea or for your dinner. (Tea, obviously.) I've spent most of my life in Scotland, but with an English mum, a Northern Irish dad and a couple of formative years in Wales, I'm not always sure where different bits of my mongrel vocabulary come from. I shamelessly abused Facebook to find out what words different friends use, with my feed full of contextless questions, from 'Leash or lead?' to:

Me: What do you call pajama-type clothes which you specifically have for wearing round the house?

Anne: Either still pajamas, or 'lounge-wear' or my 'comfy clothes' or my 'around the house clothes'

Tessa: Something I've noticed about this time is how I have no 'house clothes' – not even a slipper! So I have no name for them either. My granny always wore her 'house coat' though .

Annabel: Oh, the horror of the housecoat! Will we ever get old enough to wear one?! I hope not.

Some responses were fairly clear-cut; living room is on the whole more Scottish, sitting room more typical for the south of England. Other questions prompted answers which weren't directly useful but sparked off associations which took me in the right direction. This was during the height of lockdown, and perhaps by virtue of their being Covid-free posts, my notifications were full of engaged responses, helping me to fill in a linguistic map of the UK and beyond.

On which note: the bulk of my work on *The Peacock* happened during the strictest phases of lockdown in Scotland. Translating is often thought of as a solitary activity, but for me it was translation which kept me sane, in a constant dialogue not only with Isabel, and with my ever-helpful friends, but also with the characters, allowing me to escape into a world where the worst that happened was – well...

Annie Rutherford